The Sea
Les Traveled
From Hell to Margaritaville

BY CAPTAIN LES PENDLETON

For Heidi
Fellow New Berner.

Essie Press

Tailwinds –

ESSIE PRESS

Palm Coast Services, Inc.d/b/a Essie Press

Contact Essie Press at
P.O. Box 6684
Raleigh, North Carolina 27628-6684
Or
Email Address: <essie-press@lespendleton.com>
Phone: 919 632-9748

Printed in the United States of America

First Printing 2002

Cover Photo Credit

"The images used herein were obtained from
IMSI's Master Photos Collection,
1895 Francisco Blvd. East, San Rafael, CA 94901-5506,
USA."

Library of Congress Registration Number: TXu000979535

This book is dedicated to Susanne Harrison Pendleton

"MISS ESSIE"

Who changed the course of not just my small ship, Calypso, but my entire life as well.

Special Thanks

Essie's Crew - Shannon and Stephen

Cappy's crew - Alan, Chris, Kelly and Maddie

Ron and Connie Cousino

Larry and Linda Jo Basden

Lawyer Larry (Larry Economos)

Dennis and Joan Alldridge

Eddy and Jennifer Parker (and Sarah)

Henry and Brenda Heath

Pat Tilson

John and Sami Bills

Jim Grimshaw

Dennis Hopper

Bob and Deborah Leisey

Melinda Katz

Stuart and Shelia Stovall

Vinny Chianese and Sandy Foster

Martin Barrie and Darlene Satifka

John and Brenda Kitson

About the Book........

Les Pendleton and his wife Susanne live in North Carolina. Les is a retired film maker who worked on over fifty feature films during his twenty year career. You will see his name in the credits for movies such as LAST OF THE MOHICANS, BLUE VELVET, NO MERCY, SUPER MARIO BROTHERS and many others. He retired to write movie scripts in 1992 only to find that he preferred the less structured world of novels.

In June of 1999 Les was preparing to head south for the winter aboard his 38' Irwin sloop, BeginAgin. He had been divorced for about three years and wanted to finally take the trip he had his heart set on since his teens. However, in August of that same year, he met Susanne Curtis and all plans changed. Kindred spirits with the same fire for adventure, Susanne took to sailing instantly. They soon created a three-year plan to take the trip south together. At present, they are one year from that goal. In October of 2003 they will head down the ICW towards Margaritaville and hope that the story you have just read pales in comparison to their journey.

Ninety five percent of what is said in THE SEA LES TRAVELED is true. Events have been moved around a little for continuity sake, real characters have switched places in actual events and a very few tales are totally fiction but felt (in Les's troubled mind) to be real. All of the photos are real and the actual names are correct, both people and boats.

Les has been sailing about a half century on a succession of boats starting with an eleven foot Penguin on the James River in Newport News, Virginia to his current Gulfstar 43 named Last Dance. Along the way, he has acquired his 100 Ton USCG Master's License and sailed most of the mid Atlantic coastline from Maryland to Florida. Today, Last Dance is sailed nearly every weekend on the Neuse River and Pamlico Sound with the same endearing cast of characters you will be introduced to in this book.

So, if you love sailboats and cruising, you have come to the right place. Pull up a chair, put a log on the fire, open a Corona or perhaps a hot cup of coffee with a shot of Bailey's in it and sit back. Let your mind wander and accompany Cappy and Essie aboard Calypso as they follow the path of the wind to points south.

A Night Sail on Last Dance

A 'mostly' true tale

Chapter One

I finally had to admit to myself that my life was near terminally flawed. I was forty-six years old, hopelessly mired in a marriage to a woman who had forgotten that I was actually a living breathing life-form. I had long ago become just the lawn mowing, overweight, boring, tuition providing necessity that pissed off the kids and did nothing for her libido. My job sucked beyond all of the nightmares I had as a child of growing up like my dad. I was in a living Hell consisting only of getting up, going to my despised job and coming home, all amidst a throng of tens of thousands of other lost souls, far too angry to be behind the wheel of a car. Together we formed the largest, most aggressive army in the world. All of us were trying to win a spot in an endless line of traffic, to be at least one foot in front of the gladiator behind. We just wanted a chance to scream "I won, you bastard!" if only for a fleeting moment of victory.

I guess under all of this there was a remnant of love. Actually, I was sure my kids still loved me, they were just busy preparing to enter the battlefield themselves and God only knows there was no room for compassion in a mind so soon to be thrown into the fray. My wife, on the other hand, must have grown to hate me. I slept upstairs, on the floor of the unfurnished addition that seemed so critical to our existence just two years and forty thousand bucks ago. Lately, I had taken to staying late at work, then driving to the mall and sitting on a bench for two hours, finally taking the hour drive home that should get me there just after she had turned in for the night. We truly couldn't stand to talk to each other. I don't know how two, basically decent people, both of whom loved their kids to the limit, could be so bad to one another. I was past worrying about a reason for how we got here or even trying to find a cure for our situation. I just needed out. I had been biding my time till the kids were out of the house. Heard that before? Finally, the oldest son was already married and divorced, twenty five years old and getting older by the hour. He was well entrenched in his own war zone, the polished mahogany and stainless steel beach-heads of a billion dollar plus corporate war. The middle son was finally deciding after seven years and no degree, that he probably didn't need to be in college. The baby, my only daughter, had already been a sniper for four years, only her enemy was her mother. She had effectively disabled the foe and was passing her days as a college freshman. At least, none of them needed a roof at home any longer and none of them appeared to have any interest in being there for much over an hour at the most. So, it was now just a huge catacomb where our coffins stayed nestled in the native soil till we returned in the wee hours of night to hide from one another and the world. I had had enough! And, so I left!

It didn't really matter where I was going at the time. The only place I really felt comfortable was inside the cabin of my small sloop, Calypso. She was old, only thirty nine feet long, but she was my sanctuary. She was comfortably berthed in her slip in New Bern, a small coastal North Carolina town about two hours east of Hell, that is, Raleigh, where I was leaving my problems to solve themselves. I think the highlight of the past twenty-five years was my last morning there. I hadn't really determined exactly when I was running away. I was like a car with the motor running, sitting in the driveway during a thunderstorm, waiting for a break in the torrential rain, or for my owner to make a break for it and run towards me. The break in the rain came on the morning of October 8th. It was just another Monday, and I couldn't do it any longer. I was sitting at my desk, staring at a computer screen. I hadn't added a sentence to the report I was writing in over two weeks. My heart and mind had already left, it was only a matter of time till my body followed. Dalton Smythewicke, my sickeningly British supervisor, appeared over my shoulder. I knew what was coming and I was going to savor every tasteful morsel of it.

"Les, I have to ask you, exactly what are you working on? I haven't seen a progress report or a work statement from you in several weeks. You know, employee evaluations are coming up and you DON'T want me to have to come down on you, do you? The job market is getting fairly tight around here and you have quite a load on your plate, don't you?"

"Well, Dalton" I said, glee obviously exploding on my face, "you are the only LOAD that I have on my plate. And to tell you the truth, I think I'm just going to scrape you off into the waste basket where you belong, you stupid, self-righteous, sanctimonious piece of shit. You are not only the biggest single asshole I've ever known, no one here can stand to look at your fat, ugly face, your obese, deformed body or be exposed to your constant body odor and bad breath. You are going to have to make due with riding herd on some other mindless slob from here on out, or for that matter, just go back into the corner of your own disgusting little cubicle and jack off. You're fired, Smythewicke! I no longer have need of your services as my employer. And one other thing, go screw yourself!"

With a tirade that strong, amongst the crowd of my fellow workers, I had forced the move on myself. My career at Carolina Bible Manufacturing was most certainly over.

I drove home leisurely, stopping extra long at every light and smiling at the poor bastards on all sides of me blaring their horns at me for impeding ten seconds of their progress to and from different stations in Hell. I was leaving. I was OUTTA HERE. Everything around me suddenly looked different. I even noticed that there were trees along the road to my house, something that had totally escaped me over the past dozen years or so. They were really nice. I made a mental note to go climb one at my first opportunity. Maybe I'd go roll in some freshly cut grass, now there was something I really enjoyed as a kid.

The house was empty. The wife was still working. She taught six graders how to leave their guns at home and not set the school buildings on fire. The cause of actually teaching the little bastards to read and write had long since been given over to more relevant and worldly concerns. I was going to miss the old farm house. I had loved it from the day I discovered it's unheated, unplumbed, uninsulated, hundred year old skeleton sitting in the midst of a wonderful grove of pecan trees. For me, it was love at first sight. I had slaved to restore it to its former glory and create for myself, my own version of Tara, complete with a wrap around, columned porch and thirteen foot ceilings. It might have worked if I had moved the kids out into the country sooner. Instead, it instilled in these creatures of the city, a rabid disdain for all things rural and me in particular for forcing them into life in an episode of Green Acres. The wife took their side and my retreat from Hell quickly became another room in it. Well, it was over today. I sat down at my desk and typed out the following note on the computer.

"Dearest,

I can't do this anymore. I'm leaving. Everything here is yours. I have taken four hundred dollars out of the bank, one credit card (the bad one with only a five hundred buck limit) and left the rest. Sell, move, keep it all or throw it away as you wish. I wish you the best in all you do and I think my not being here will be a blessing for all of you.

Les".

I got back in the car and headed to New Bern. I suppose I should have been sad, but I couldn't seem to bring forward any emotion other than relief. I had never been a corporate team player. In all matters business, I was a loser. It was just about ten PM when I finally made the coast. The entire city took on a different look this evening. I knew the town was still the same, it was me who had changed. Most probably, I would never look at anything the same. I was too dead inside to even have remorse about leaving anything or anybody behind. The only thing I seemed to be feeling was excitement at the prospects of my rebirth. I pulled the car alongside the curb in front of my favorite tavern, Captain Ratty's Bar and Grill. I sat for a moment in the front seat of the car, wondering if anyone would notice a difference in me. I took off the tie that still lay half noosed around my neck and threw it out the door into the rain drenched street. Then, smiling at seeing it's quickly soaking carcass lying there, slammed the door shut and went into the rustic, cedar and brass interior where I knew friendly faces awaited. Being a weeknight, it was not full and I recognized most of the people inside as regular customers.

Captain Ratty's - New Bern, N.C. A great place

"Les, what are you doing in town on a Monday?"

The proprietor, Captain Ratty himself was a close friend. Actually, his name was Tom and he and his wife Deborah had come to New Bern for many of the same reasons I had, looking for a better way of spending the time allotted to them on the planet.

Everyone at the boat was friendly. I always assumed this was because when people were at their boats, they were in a good mood. The last thing they wanted to think about when they were here is how bad things were at home. Sure, there were a few elbow bending, beer stained evenings when a buddy would have one too many and unload the truth of their situation to me, and whoever else was within earshot. The nature of these confessions was always strikingly similar to my own situation but the sordid tales were generally told as if they were some sort of ultra confidential life situation that would ruin the teller if others found out.

Was everyone's life just as screwed up as mine? It certainly seemed to be the case. And yet, as problematic as each of our own stories were, in New Bern, the world was warm and friendly.

New Bern was an old town, named after Bern, Switzerland from where it's founders had sojourned, hundreds of years before. It had a very European look and charm that was nowhere else to be found in the South from my observations. It was truly an oasis in the wilderness. Nestled on the banks of the Neuse River, it offered spectacular views of the water and for that matter, a mind warming view of a watery path to adventure, excitement and life, a path I would soon be on. This was a pretty heady night for me. I took my seat at the bar and offered Tom my explanation for a weekday appearance.

"Captn. Tom", as I called him. It was easier to remember after six or so beers. "You are the first to witness a dead man coming to life".

"What the hell you talkin' about, Les? You get a big promotion or somethin'?"

"Or somethin' pretty well covers it, Captain. Today," I paused and took a breath. I wanted to hear the words coming out of my own mouth, myself. I wanted to know if I sounded relieved, scared or just insane. "Today, I left my job, my wife, my family, everything. I'm going to straighten up Calypso a little and then, well, then I'm headed south. First the Keys, then the Bahamas, maybe even as far as South America. Hell, I don't know, I don't even care. I'm running away you might say. Hit me with a tall draft. And keep 'em coming till I tell you to stop."

"You're shitting me, Les. What has come over you? A fight with the old lady? I know you don't get along any too well."

"I guess I've just come to the realization that if I'm not happy with me, how can I possibly expect anyone else to be. I'm going to change that."

I hadn't paid any attention to the man sitting one stool down from me at the bar. He had evidently been listening with some interest to my story.

"You know, mate, if-n' I were a mind to go, I'd sure make a wonderful addition to your little expedition, voyage, whatever the hell you're doing."

Somewhat, (OK, more than somewhat) totally suspicious, I countered,

"and that would be what sort of an addition?"

He toyed with his unkempt beard as he spoke, staring up at the ceiling as if there was some sort of display there that only he could see.

"The sea can be a mighty desolate place for a fellow to be looking to if he's wanting some peace. I've seen it when no man alive would want to be out there. I've been scared plumb out of my wits. Not something for an inexperienced Captain to try. I could be a big help out there when it starts to get shitty."

"I assume, by your comments that you have a lot of off-shore experience?"

"That's right, Cappy. Been at sea most of my life."

"Where are you from? Gloucester, Nova Scotia, where?"

"Born in Des Moines, actually. Felt a craving, a longing for the sea early on. After a short stint in prison, I decided that I needed to go exercise my fantasies of a long sea voyage. Been at it ever since."

"Prison? What were you in for?"

"Ah, nothing serious. I was behind in alimony to my fourth wife and I made the mistake of trying to float a check for a few days to cover her. Anyway, it bounced and she had my ass put in the hoosegow. Hey, I'm glad she did. It got me started on my way to where I am now, and a hell of a lot happier than I've ever been. You can relate to that now, can't you? What with you leaving your wife and all."

"I guess so, though I can't imagine being in prison."

"You can't, huh? Most of my marriages were a lot tougher than prison. Anyway, I think you're going to need somebody like me if you're serious about heading offshore."

"Why is that? I've been sailing for years."

"Offshore?"

"Well not really, but I've been caught in some bad weather over the years."

"If it wasn't offshore bad weather, you ain't been caught in no bad weather. Wasn't, was it?"

"Well, not really, I guess."

"There you have it. Yeah, I've seen it all out there. Remember the big one back in 92'? That's the one they made the movie about."

"Yeah, what about it?"

"I was there, Skip. Yep, right in the middle of the whole dadblamed mess."

"Let's get this straight. You're saying you were on a boat in the middle of, THE PERFECT STORM?"

"Won't none too perfect from where I was sitting, there in

the fo'castle of the Adrian Gains, a fishing boat out of Gloucester."

"That sounds a lot like the Andrea Gail, the one that was the main boat in the book. And, they never mentioned any Adrian Gains" I said with a disbelieving slur to my voice.

"Well, Skip, all those boats have similar names. Just the same, we were out there. The writer only talked about the boats that had some sort of a happy ending."

"The Andrea Gail sunk, everybody on board drowned. That's a happy ending?"

"Well, the Adrian Gains fiasco was a complete disaster. Yeah, the Coast Guard won't be braggin' about that."

"What happened? She sunk too?"

"Far worsener than that, Cappy, far scarier story. Wanna' buy me another beer and I'll tell you all about it."

"Capn' Matty, set em up here again, looks like a long night is about to get started."

I have to admit, this old salt could tell a mean story, though he never actually got into the retelling of the details of the mysterious Adrian Gains. He said he was just too torn up at the time to get into it and replaced it with a number of equally unbelievable stories. Finally, he got back around to selling me on the idea of taking him with me.

"So, it's settled. You need a mate like me. Now, what about a cook?"

"A cook? Jeez, my boat is only thirty-nine feet long. I don't think I need a cook."

"Captn', my best advice to you as First Mate is to get a cook. When you're cold and wet, exhausted plum down to your toes, nothing, absolutely nothing beats a hot plate of food served up by a fine looking woman."

"A woman? I'm not taking along a woman. Hell, that's the sort of problem I'm trying to get away from."

"Now Cappy, sure, you're a little hot under the brow right now, but come the first blow, you're gonna' be right glad that ole John Silver come along with you, you will."

"That wouldn't be Long John Silver, would it by chance?"

"You've heard of me, huh?"

"You have to be kidding. Long John Silver, friend, as in TREASURE ISLAND, was a notorious pirate. He was a fictional scoundrel. That's probably the worst name you could use to get signed onboard somebody's boat for a cruise, don't you think?"

"He was a character in a book? Damn! I never heard that before."

"Jeez, maybe I'm mistaken. Never mind. So, what makes you think this woman would even want to come with us and cook? Calypso is not a big luxury yacht or anything. She's sound, yes, but a heavy, older style thirty-nine footer. There's not a lot of room for a woman to store her crap and to tell you the truth, I'm a little tired of women in my life right now."

"I understand completely, Cappy. Tell you what, she only lives a block or so from here. Whatd'ya say we go by her place right now and ask her?"

By now, my judgment was undoubtedly being clouded to some extent by the continuous stream of draft beer that had been accompanying John Silver's outrageous tales. I couldn't really tell you which made the other go down easier, whether the beer made the words more palatable to swallow or the tales made the beer seem more necessary. Whichever, I was certainly falling under some sort of spell, wielded by this madcap character.

"Captain Ratty, the check please."

"Tell you what Les, tonight's on me. But, don't show up here again next week and tell me you've changed your mind. I'd have to charge you double. Besides, you practically put this place on the map down here. Drop me a postcard from some exotic spot this winter. Good luck!"

The coastal mist was settling quickly on the quaint, cobblestone streets as I walked with John Silver to meet Susanne Curtis, known to her friends as Essie, referring to her initials, I suppose. It's funny, at the moment when things are occurring in your life, they often times don't seem as significant as they, in fact, are. Today, looking back on that night, I have to say it was a major turning point on the road that my future was to travel.

"Essie lived in the historical section of town. Generally, these apartments were upstairs, over the top of stores and offices with an alley between them. Entrance to the apartments was from narrow sets of steps that touched down either in the alley or behind the store. Such was the case at Essie's. We started down the alley; each step bringing more darkness as the streetlight in front of the building became progressively distant. The stairs were just a dark shadow in front of us when the distinct sound of breaking glass shattered the stillness directly overhead, showering us with a heavy rain of broken glass. In the midst of all the falling shards, a large framed picture came spinning to Earth, crashing only two feet from my hunched over frame, which was trying to dodge the onslaught. The alley was also bathed in a new light, coming from the now open hole in the wall above us where a curtained window had been only moments before. The light reflected clearly off the shattered glass and a now crumpled picture of none other than Broadway Joe Namath, in his Jet's uniform. Obviously, it was a sacrament used in some sort of hero worship. As we tried to make sense of what had just occurred, a shrill voice began to fill the otherwise quiet setting.

"You lazy, stupid moron! You haven't done a damn thing in two months but watch football and now you ask me when I'm going to clean up your empty beercans? I'll tell you when, when your nose-hair reaches your friggin knees, that's when. And if you go get that picture and try and hang it in the living room again, I swear I'll be gone so fast you'll be talking to my shadow."

"Is that right, you aggravating bitch? And where do you think you'll go, back to your Momma's trailer? I'm sure she'll be thrilled with that news."

"I'll tell you where, Bud-belly, I'll hitch a ride on a boat headed south and just move to the Caribbean, permanently!"

"Hitch a ride on somebody's yacht, huh? Just like that? You're friggin' dreaming! Who'd be dumb enough to take along a human buzzsaw?"

John Silver's voice poignantly interrupted the special moment that was in progress upstairs.

"Yo, Essie, you want to sign onboard a yacht for a trip south to the Bahamas? Be gone all winter."

Essie looked over at the bewildered man, beer in one hand, the other rubbing his fat belly. He could barely believe that his question could be answered so quickly, at two in the morning.

"Don't ask if you don't like the answer, Earl. I'll be leaving now. Have a great evening. And, oh yeah, you're out of beer.

You might want to check with the Salvation Army in the morning."

It seemed like only seconds before a duffel bag came flying through the same opening that Willy Joe had sailed from only moments before. The door opened at the top of the stairs and a smallish, dark haired woman began her descent into the alley. The dim light from the window showed her to be about thirty-eight years or so, with a pleasant face, trim athletic build and a very brisk hustle to her step. The "I don't take no bullshit from anybody" body language was overly apparent in her every movement. She had another small bag in her hand, which she handed to John Silver as she picked up the duffel bag from the ground. I had to wonder if she just kept these bags packed for such scenarios as this, and just how often something like this had occurred in her life. From her nonchalant attitude, it didn't appear to be a traumatic event.

"Long John, how the hell are ya?"

"Jus fine, Essie. Great to have you aboard."

"This our skipper?"

"Yup, this here's Captain...Well, I'll be damn, Cappy. I don't guess I've gotten your name yet."

I formerly extended my hand to Essie.

"Les, Les Pendleton."

"What kind of boat you got, Captain?"

"An old Pearson, a 39 foot cutter rig."

"I know them, a good old boat. She'll take a lot of water in stride. Got a pretty decent galley."

"I'm real happy with her."

"We staying on board her tonight? Or at least what's left of it?"

"I guess so, I haven't got any other place to sleep."

John and Essie replied almost in concert, "me neither, let's go."

I was too tired by this point in the evening to even consider the ramifications of taking on a crew so quickly and without knowing either of them. Given time and resumes, I would undoubtedly have chosen neither, however, with my limited budget and the fact that neither even mentioned money, I was willing to take the risk that they might be a third of what John Silver had intimated. We walked back to Captain Ratty's, hopped in my car and headed to the marina. In short order, the three of us had staked claims to our berths. As Captain, I had an unquestionable claim on the large aft cabin, though I really felt bad about not letting the woman have it. Call me old-fashioned. Besides, all my belongings were already stowed away there. I quickly got into the buff, as I loved to sleep butt naked in the aft cabin. As I sat on the edge of the berth, I took out my wallet and checked the contents, which constituted every cent I had to leave on. After filling up and getting a burger on the drive down, I had a grand total of three hundred seventy-two dollars and a few pennies. Coupled with the five hundred-buck limit on my credit card, I was leaving with only eight hundred seventy-two bucks. I took the cash and card and stuffed them in the small Tupperware, watertight jar I kept on the shelf just over the bunk.

I had to be on the edge of madness, but yet, I just felt, no, KNEW I was doing the right thing. In moments, Captain and crew had passed out. All in all, it was a pretty damned interesting day.

Chapter Two

Even before I was fully awake, I could feel the pounding above my eyes reminding me that my three-beer limit had been exceeded the evening before. There was a chill in the cabin. Even in this condition, I thought to myself, there is nothing better than sleeping in a small boat. The slight motion of the hull, the gentle lapping sound caused by tiny ripples, even in a still harbor. I truly felt at home and at peace with the world on board Calypso. Though it was early October, the Carolina mornings were starting to have a touch of fall in them. It was one of those times when you know you should get up and answer the call of your bladder but you're too tired, too hung-over, and far too warm and snug where you are to make any drastic changes. I lay still, not wanting to exert any un-needed pressure on my water tank and thought over the evening's events. My God, there's two people on this boat besides me! It all came rushing back. Had I made a drastic mistake? In my beer clouded reasoning I had enlisted the help of two complete strangers to take Calypso in pursuit of my personal dreams. For crying out loud, one of them called himself Long John Silver! I must have been out of my gourd. Perhaps, I was just scared, afraid to put out to sea by myself. Maybe my unconscious mind knew this better than my fully awake one. No matter what the case, I had to go take a leak, immediately. As my feet hit the floor, the smell of fresh coffee seemed to float into my cabin while at the same time, a somewhat familiar woman's voice broke the silence.

"Cappy, breakfast is served. Eggs gonna' work for you this morning?"

"Just a second, please. I'm using the head. Be right there."

It was the new cook who had signed aboard a few hours ago. She obviously took her job seriously. My own head was pounding far too hard to even look at raw eggs this early.

After a much needed bladder deflation, I walked up the companionway that leads down into my aft cabin, crossed over the cockpit and back down into the main cabin where the galley and Essie were located.

"Morning, Cappy. Got your coffee right here, how do you like it?"

"Make it black, please."

"Got a some cat's hair in the mouth this morning, Cappy? How about a little Irish Cream in the coffee? That'll rake 'em out."

"That might not be a bad idea."

"And how do you want your eggs? I can do 'em most anyway, even in seaway."

"Over medium, please. Make it two and some toast if you can."

"Toast and bacon are sitting right here. Did 'em first. So, what's on the schedule? How much work does the old girl need before we can get underway?"

"As far as I'm concerned, as soon as this head of mine eases off and we can get the supplies loaded, I'm ready to shove off."

"You already had your farewell party?"

"What are you talking about?"

"You don't have any friends here?"

"Of course, I have lots of friends here."

"Then you have to throw a farewell party. It's a tradition. I'll take care of everything. You just do what you have to do to get the boat ready to go today. I'll throw together a little soiree for this evening and you can make the rounds and invite whoever you want to come over around seven this evening. I'll be asking a couple of folks I want to say good-bye to also if that's OK with you. I'm sure Long John will as well."

"Speaking of John Silver, where is he this morning?"

"Right here, Cappy. Been up at the store having coffee with the boys and splicing a few lines for you. I don't like a dead-end on no lines on a boat. Don't look seaman-like if you get my drift. Don't worry I'll get Calypso Bristol in pretty short order."

It was apparent by now that I didn't hold my booze nearly as well as either of my crew, especially when you consider the fact that they each had two drinks for every one I put away. I felt now that there was one subject I had to address.

"Guys, I guess it was me that failed to mention this, but about you both being crew. As much as I would love the company and the help, I don't have any money to pay a crew to come along. I've just left home myself and only have a couple hundred bucks to even leave on. I'm basically running away, you could say. I'm no different than a teenager who just isn't getting along at home. If I didn't have this boat to come to, I'd qualify as a street person, I guess."

John Silver spoke first, without a moment of hesitation.

"Not to worry, Cappy. I been running away myself, for over forty years. I never have worried about having any money. Seems like I get by OK. Just when I think to myself, "now how in the Hell am I going to eat, somebody'll come along and say, Long John, I got a little job for you. That's how it's been all these years. So, what I'm saying Cappy, is if you want me to come along, I'll find a way to it make it work. You'll just be furnishing me a place to stay in return for my services as first mate. It'll work out, you'll see."

"And Essie, what about you?"

"I haven't got anybody waiting up for me anywhere. I'm ready for an adventure. So, you have a crew. We know where we stand and that's that. Now eat your eggs before they get cold. Here, I'll warm up your coffee a little."

I guess no cheaper crew had ever been assembled since the British Navy ended conscription in the previous century.

The morning passed quickly. John Silver was proving to be very knowledgeable in the rigging, organizing, and mechanical systems of a sailboat. And, he seemed to attract people like a magnet. As he worked, either singing a somewhat R rated sea tune or whistling something from a Jimmy Buffett album, everyone who passed by would stop, watch him for a while and then just engage in conversation with him. I don't believe I had ever had that many people stop by to chat in a morning. And Essie, she busied herself making everything below livable and a Hell of a lot cleaner. Calypso had never had an interested woman on board and it showed. She was strictly utilitarian with no attention to dressing her up. That was changing quickly. She even removed the mildewed curtains that had hung above the galley ports for over ten years and took them, along with all the ship's linens, to the marina laundry room. Calypso was even starting to smell clean. This crew thing was turning out to be not such a bad an idea.

We made good use of the extra day; double checking everything and occasionally finding something previously overlooked. By late afternoon, Calypso was shipshape, stores were loaded and we were all ready for the evening's festivities. I had told most everyone on the dock to come over for an impromptu farewell party. I expected that some dozen or so friends would find their way over after the sun started to go down. It was therefore, somewhat unexpected when the first three dozen people showed up, most carrying gift-wrapped bottles of liquor or wine for us to carry with us on our way south, that is whatever they didn't drink that evening. The way they were tearing into it, I was just hoping for a wash. One thing becomes very clear when you are headed south for the winter. All sailors, serious blue water adventurers as well as bar stool dreamers, all feel left behind as a friend heads out. I've been there. I understand only too well that feeling of being stranded by someone I knew, and who had found some way out. They were happy for us, yet they were sad for themselves. They generally sucked it in however, and tried to give the best sendoff they were capable of. This evening proved to be no exception. Calypso was completely full, the overflow crowd littering the dock and neighboring boats. Stereo speakers had been moved into the cockpit and the sound of Caribbean and Latin tunes wafted across the entire marina. The cockpit of Calypso had been illuminated by a string of red chili-pepper party lights that Essie had commandeered from somewhere and I have to admit it, Essie cleaned up real nice. She was wearing a bright blue party dress, very tropical with brightly colored palm leaves for a design. She had her dark, wavy hair pulled back and her eyes literally glowed a dark greenish brown. She had a very warm smile and if I had to say it, I found her quite attractive. John Silver on the other hand, was dressed up in character for the occasion. He had a red bandanna pulled over his head like a stocking cap, pirate fashion, a blue and white striped seaman's shirt, cut-off three quarter length ragged bottom blue jeans, no shoes, and even a fake eye patch that he would pull up every time a woman passed as if to say, "I'm looking you over real good." He was built slim but wiry, had a bushy mop of hair with equally furry eyebrows and beard, all in a solid gray color. He eschewed the need for a glass and instead carried a long necked bottle of Corona with him as a constant prop, continually moving his body to the Caribbean beat. This was obviously a man who had been to a great number of boat parties.

By eleven PM, on my count, the forty or so guests and myself had consumed a dozen cases of beer, twelve bottles of wine, two carrot cakes bought special for the occasion, thrown two rowdy guests in the creek, toasted our departure at least a hundred times, and begun the final organized rendition of HAPPY TRAILS TO YOU, a tradition at our marina when neighbors were sailing off. There was more than one damp eye when wishing us well, but that can pretty much be translated as "why are you leaving me here, you bastards, and heading to paradise?" I understood only too well. By two AM, everyone save the crew of Calypso had departed. The stereo had been turned down very low and the last chorus of ONE PARTICULAR HARBOR was painting a beautiful picture in my overtaxed mind. I contemplated for just a moment that by this time, my wife would have come to the realization that I was really gone and would have called each of the kids, explaining that the world's greatest asshole had finally taken the most cowardice action of his life, by running away. That thought seemed to bring me peace. I took one last swallow of my now warm beer and settled down on my bunk for the final night in Calypso's safe, shore bound slip. Tomorrow, everything in my life would change. I would no longer be a disillusioned middle-aged man looking for some way out of a bad life situation. There would be no excuses for being unhappy from here on out. Now, the adventure would begin in earnest.

During the night, halyards began slapping up against the mast and the hull of Calypso started to move ever so slightly. The wind was beginning to build. I lay awake in my berth, wondering where the wind would be taking me over the coming months and years. It was a hypnotic sound, and music to my mind. I drifted in and out of sleep for hours, each time, upon waking, the noise of the wind was louder. If this held, tomorrow would offer an exciting ride down the Neuse River.

I was awakened by the sound of the VHF radio. The constant weather channel had been selected by one of my crew. I could hear the report indicating a small craft advisory for the Pamlico and Albemarle sounds. Since the Neuse emptied into the Pamlico, any weather report for the Pamlico lent some indication of how the weather on the river would be. The Neuse is wide and though not terribly deep, it offers a generally safe sailing depth of around twelve to fifteen feet everywhere unless marked as a shoal on the map. Conditions never get so bad on the river that Calypso couldn't go where I wanted. She was deep drafted, around five feet six with a full keel and plenty of ballast. Though not fast in light air, she was a very seaworthy, stable boat, capable of extended offshore cruises. The only things that ever concerned me on the river were the presence of thunderstorms, which could possibly offer a lightning strike, or a waterspout, the wet version of a tornado. Other than that, I didn't worry about weather on the river. If we sank, at fifteen feet of average water depth, you could just grab a seat on the spreaders, twenty feet up the mast and wait for help to arrive. The Neuse, for any seaworthy boat over thirty feet in length, was pretty much like sailing in a bathtub. This morning's advisory was not going to put a damper on the departure. With the fall chill back in the morning air, I put on my light-weight foul weather jacket, a pair of blue jeans, and deck shoes. With an adrenaline-fueled enthusiasm, I crossed over the cockpit and back into the main salon. As if on cue, Essie was fully dressed, none the worse for another night of very little sleep and a lot of wine. She was in a pleasant mood as she offered,

"Here's your coffee, Cappy. Didn't put any Irish Cream in it as some skipper's won't touch even a breath of alcohol when they're under way. Good idea, too."

"Sounds good to me Essie. And I'm not too hungry, so how about a little toast and jam?"

"Coming right up. John is topside. He said he was going to go ahead and get her ready to leave her slip and he assumed the dock-lines are ours."

"They are, and I want to take them all with us."

I wolfed down my coffee, two pieces of toast and hurried topside where I found John Silver jumping lively on the dock.

"I'm going to fire the diesel, John. How long before we're ready to shove off?"

"Five minutes on your word, Cappy."

"Prepare to shove off then, John Silver."

I went to the cockpit, hit the pre-heat button for the diesel and thirty seconds later, pressed the start button. The old Perkins jumped to life immediately, a little white smoke and water pouring out of the exhaust as was normal. After a few minutes, the smoke disappeared as the engine warmed.

"I've got the stern lines, John Silver."

"Aye, Cappy and I've got the bow. We're all clear forward."

At the last second as we pulled off, two couples, both close friends came buy the dock to see us off. Half dressed, with their coffee mugs still in their hands, one wife still wrapped up in a blanket, they waved and wished us fair winds as we backed from our slip and slowly made our way out of the security and confines of the marina. We were on our way. This felt different than any departure I'd ever made, though I had sailed all my life. I'd always been tied to the land, knowing I couldn't go further than where I could return from in just a few days, so as to be able to fulfil my land duties as employee, husband and father. Those ties all gone, I was headed out to an indefinite destination and an uncertain course. Calypso was headed south, that's all that really mattered. As the small waters of Northwest Creek emptied into the two mile wide Neuse, I looked back one last time and saw our friends still on the dock, watching us get smaller. I waved again, an exaggerated motion I felt sure they could see, and they responded in kind. It was kind of sad in a way. We made the turn to port into the river, the marina disappeared from view and the wind picked up to a steady twenty-five knots. John and Essie had joined me in the cockpit, where the spray dodger and bimini top protected us considerably from the chilly wind. It was time to put up sail. The wind was from our starboard quarter and would offer us a fast broad reach down the river.

"John, I'll head her upwind, you raise the main with a double reef tucked in her, then we'll use the staysail only. No need to kill ourselves or strain the old girl. We can make a steady six knots and you and Essie can get to know the feel of her."

"Aye, Cappy, head her up."

I turned Calypso upriver, into the wind and set the autopilot to hold that course. John Silver expertly double-reefed the mainsail as I raised it with the cockpit-mounted winch. All of the lines on Calypso were led to the cockpit so that she could be single-handed in most any weather. Generally, I had to sail a lot by myself, making an autopilot and all lines being led to the cockpit a necessity. After the main reached its spot on the mast and I secured the halyard, I released the auto-pilot, turned to port and watched as the strong northeasterly wind filled the sail and Calypso began to heel. Calypso immediately responded and the hull speed jumped to four knots.

"Ok, John Silver, unfurl the staysail. That should get us up to hull speed."

John immediately did as requested. Calypso answered with another five degrees of heel as she settled into her favorite slot. As expected, she easily attained six and half knots and started a gentle rocking motion, acknowledging the three foot chop stirred up by the strong winds running along with us downriver. By now, the sun was coming up nicely and it was conceivable that the weatherman's prediction of a high temperature of sixty-five would be on target. The sun's bright rays hitting on the surface of the water created a pattern of sparkles that reminded me of angel-hair on a Christmas tree. It ran in silver streaks from our hull straight back to the rising sun. Still, with twenty-five knots of wind, the chill factor made standing in the cockpit with the side curtains up, a chilly ride. As if she had read my mind, Essie appeared on the companionway steps with a cup of steaming coffee in her hand.

"Here you go, Cappy, this will warm you right up."

"Essie, you're making me wonder how I ever cruised without a ship's cook on board. You're spoiling me."

"I just want to earn my keep. When we hit those crystal clear, tropical waters and you don't need a cup of coffee, just remember this morning. Cause then, I'll be snorkeling before you even wake up."

"God, that sounds incredible. Keep talking to me like that. I love it when you trop-talk."

John Silver sat down beside me, noticing my steaming cup.

"And does the First Mate qualify for a cup?"

"Already poured and sitting on the galley counter, John Silver. Damn, you're an impatient one."

"Me? I'm just efficient, Essie. There ain't nothin' pushy about me. Now, can I have that cup of java?"

"I'll give it to you alright, old man."

Essie laughed as she went back down the companionway steps for John Silver's cup. She had an easy way about her and fit in very well in a man's world without giving up one bit of femininity. She also looked pretty damned good in those too tight jeans she had on this morning. Nothing like sailing to keep a person fit. I had always wished my wife had an interest in boats. I truly believed that if she would have just occasionally been willing to go sailing with me, we'd probably still be together. Of course, the reality was, I'd probably still be slumped over at my desk with Dalton breathing down my neck. God, it was worth everything just to not have to be there ever again.

"Hey Cappy, there's a good sized ketch headed out behind us. Looks like they're coming our way. Anybody you recognize?"

I picked up my binoculars from the teak gear tray mounted on the steering pedestal and focused them on the vessel, which by now had her sails up and was heeling over as she built up speed.

"It' Island Time, a Morgan 41 OutIsland that belongs to good friends from the marina, Larry and Linda Jo. I'm surprised to see them out this early. I'll just give a shout on the radio and see where they're headed. You remember them don't you? He was the guy at the party last night that you said drank an entire keg of beer."

"Oh yeah, I can hardly believe he's up and about after last night. Man, he put some away."

I punched in channel 16 on the VHF ship's radio.

"Island Time, Island Time, this is Calypso calling." Larry answered back,

"This is Island Time, switch and answer channel sixty-eight."

"Good morning, Island Time. I'm surprised to see you guys out here this early after such a late, and rowdy evening."

"Well, you're right, but Linda Jo and I got to thinking about you shoving off without us and we couldn't even sleep. So, we decided to get up and sail along beside you for awhile today. You know, at least pretend we're headed south for a few hours.

Island Time - Sailing with us to Ocracoke

Will you humor us and let us sail alongside, at least to Oriental?"

"No problem guys, I really wish you were coming along the entire trip with us. No party will be the same without the dauntless crew of Island Time. We'll ease the sheets a little till you catch up."

"With this wind, it won't be long. God, I love this kind of sailing. Island Time is like a cinderblock with sails and this is what she loves."

"Roger, we'll be here waiting for you. Calypso back to sixteen."

I turned to Essie and John, smiling as I spoke.

"I know just how they feel. Every since I've had a boat, whenever a friend took off on a cruise, I felt like I was being deserted. It's just been burning, eating out my insides all this time, to be doing just what we're doing this morning. I can sympathize with them. I should have done this ten years ago. Damn, look at Island Time move. Those old Morgans love the wind, just about like Calypso. Her waterline's a little longer than us, so she can probably outrun us by a bit."

We all sat back in the cockpit. Calypso was once again steering herself with the autopilot. The sky was clear, the wind strong and the Neuse was as beautiful as ever I had seen her. I was in a good boat with a good crew. I had no clue how I was going to make this work, how I would make enough money to keep going. All I knew was, this is where I wanted to be. I was doing what I wanted, no NEEDED to be doing and everything would have to just work the way it was going to. I was no longer going to be a leaf in a windstorm. I would stand my ground to at least attempt to achieve a small part of what I had dreamed about for most of my life.

Island Time slowly moved up on us, and by the time we had reached the Minnesott Ferry crossing, she was alongside of us. We could talk to Larry and Linda Jo without screaming, as the two boats sailed along within thirty feet of each other.

"John, turn on the cockpit speakers and let's have a little traveling music. I think a little Buffett would be in order right about now. Essie, tell me when the sun is over the yardarm."

"What the hell does that mean, Cappy?"
John Silver answered her.

"After noon, Essie, elbow bending time."

"Alright, I get the message. Will do, Cappy. I think that maybe I'll grab a little chips and salsa and, how about a chicken salad sandwich? I've got a great little bowl of it that Deal's store sells in New Bern. Thought you guys might enjoy it."

"Stop it, you're making me hungry and it's two hours till lunch. How about a refill on my coffee?"

"Coming up, Cappy."

As she went below to fetch the pot, music began to fill the air and every one was soon singing Mother, Mother Ocean, along with Jimmy B.

God, it was a spectacular site. Both boats had their flags standing out straight and their sails tight. Island Time had a bow wave being pushed up in front of her and both boats were leaving a path of white foam behind them as they screamed down the river towards Oriental. The smiles on everyone's face told the entire story.

It was only eleven AM and we were closing fast on Oriental. As much as I loved the town, and it is truly a special place, we were making such great time that I really didn't want to stop. There's a little cafe there that has the most unique atmosphere and best food you could ever hope for. It was a small white framed house that had been converted by Dave and Marsha, a great sailing couple that had just sailed into port there on their own boat and couldn't bare to leave. They rented a house, installed a small kitchen and a bar, the rest is history. Five years later, you're lucky to get a seat. And sailing stories? My God, you will eventually hear every tale and meet everybody that ever held a tiller in M&Ms. But, I had cruised to Oriental almost constantly the past five years and used it as my "pretend you've gone somewhere" destination. That's not what was happening this time. During this moment of indecision, Calypso was hailed over the VHF.

"Calypso, Calypso, Island Time calling."

"Switch and answer sixty-eight, Island Time."

"Larry, what's up? You getting ready to turn around and go home?"

"Nope, I've talked it over with Linda Jo and we're taking two days off and following you guys for a while longer. Where are you headed? Putting in at Oriental?"

"That's a negative, Larry."

And then inspiration struck me. I knew where I wanted to be tonight.

"Island Time, let's keep going straight across the sound and spend the night and tomorrow in Ocracoke. What do you say to that?"

"Les, it's blowing pretty hard right here in the river, the rollers are about four feet high now. You don't think it could get nasty out there?"

"Well, Larry, that's why I'm not sailing a sunfish. If your old Morgan even hiccups going across, I'd be surprised."

"If Calypso goes, we go."

"OK, Let's do it. We'll be waiting for you at the Anchorage Marina right there in Silver Lake. We'll have the pina-colladas ready for you when you get in."

"Waiting for us? I don't think so. We'll give you a hand with your lines when you get in."

"That sounds an awful lot like you have thrown the gauntlet there, Island Time."

Captain Larry and Linda Jo Basden

"Call it what you will, Calypso. And, if you would, tell me how far behind me you can still read the letters on our stern. Island Time back to sixteen."

"John Silver, unfurl the remainder of the headsail if you would, sir. Let's maintain a due east heading to the Island."

"Aye, aye, Cappy. Ocracoke Island it is."

As the large headsail unfurled, Calypso laid over a couple more degrees and the increase in her speed was obvious. She was now at full hull speed, or as the old salts would say, 'she had a bone in her teeth'."

The Pamlico Sound is a huge, shallow inland sea. It lies between the mainland of North Carolina and a very narrow, fragile finger of land called the outer banks that run almost entirely down the coast of the state. These spectacular outlying fingers have survived countless hurricanes and nor'easters and it was now to be seen whether or not they had what it would take to survive the myriad numbers of tourists that flocked to see these pristine pieces of Heaven. Ocracoke Island was one of these small barrier islands. The Pamlico Sound, though totally landlocked, is very large and due to an average depth of about eighteen feet, can get very choppy in a blow. About seventy miles long and thirty miles wide, when you are in the middle, you can't see land in any direction. If the visibility is low and the weather turns nasty, it can be a pretty scary place. If the wind comes out of the north-east with any strength, called a 'nor'easter', the waves can build over the full length of the Sound and become very steep and close together, a bad combination to sail against. When offshore, in the ocean, a large swell of fifteen and even over twenty feet can actually be a quite comfortable ride, if they're not breaking and sufficiently far apart. In the sound, however, a six-foot chop can pound even a strong forty-foot boat such as Calypso, to where you would not want to be onboard. During rare conditions, I'm told that waves there can exceed ten feet. If that should occur, a boat, which needs five foot of water to float, risks the possibility of bottoming-out or striking bottom between the large waves. That could be disastrous. I would never venture out when that possibility existed.

As the afternoon progressed, the winds also increased. The small craft advisory that had been issued the previous evening was right on target. Fortunately, the wind and waves were off the starboard quarter, and though the boats were rolling considerably, they were handling it admirably. Ocracoke is a ten-hour sail from New Bern and we were still a good three hours out when the winds really started to kick up. The swells built to about six feet and in my best guess, the wind was steady at thirty knots with gusts pushing forty or more. Island Time had reduced sail to her mizzen sail and small working jib. We had the main double reefed and just a postage stamp of the headsail unfurled. Both boats were exceeding hull speed as they surfed down the faces of the very steep short waves. Most of the time, they would come down off one wave and punch through the face of the next as they were very close together. Both boats have full cockpit enclosures. Otherwise, this would be one cold, wet ride. The spray dodger was staying perpetually drenched, blocking the cold water from the cockpit. We were rolling considerably and the autopilot could no longer hold the wheel. John and I were taking turns holding Calypso on course with the thirty-six inch pedestal wheel.

"Well, Cappy, we wanted wind, we got wind. The water out here has so much white spray on it, looks like it's snowing! I tell you what, I'm ready to be there."

"Shouldn't be too long before we see the stacks, John and I guarantee you I'll be at the Jolly Roger ten minutes after we tie up. I need a hamburger and a beer."

The stacks were the remnants of a dredge that sunk at the

mouth of the Ocracoke channel many years prior. They were just alongside the ferry channel and when they came clearly into view, you could feel reasonably assured that the worst was over and you would be in port in just a short while. I was anxious for them to appear and was trying to keep a sharp eye out for them. With so much spray on the water, our visibility was dropping to less than two hundred yards. This was the worst set of conditions I had experienced in all the years I had been sailing the Pamlico. I was beginning to get a little anxious for the stacks to appear. Essie mounted the steps and cheerfully offered...

"Boys, I've got some cheese and crackers and a beer for each of you. Is this great, or what?"

Her confidence in her crew lowered the anguish factor considerably.

"Thanks, Essie, I need a beer right now."

"I figured you might, I'll do a partial revocation of the no alcohol rule for just one beer. How much further, Cappy?"

"We haven't seen the stacks yet. What does the GPS say, John? I have the channel listed as BF for Big Foot Slough. Just mark it with the cursor and hit the NAV button. John starting punching in the appropriate keys and within seconds, modern technology had the answer, though not the one I wanted to hear.

"It says, 'batteries low'", sneered John.

"Where do we keep the triple 'A's?"

"Jeez, if we have any, they're in the top left drawer under the nav station, but I don't feel good about our chances of finding any. I had them on my list and forgot to pick some up. Look, just give Island Time a shout and get a fix from them."

John moved to the radio and raised Island Time.

"Larry, how far to the stacks? Our GPS is not working."

"Two point eight miles. Were averaging at least eight knots. We should be on them in about fifteen minutes max. Keep your heading at 86 degrees due East. We'll take the lead 'cause to tell you the truth, we might not see the stacks till we're right on top of them with visibility this bad, and the shoals are right beside them. I'm going to stay to the port side of the stacks at least fifty yards. You stay close and we'll lead you home. Hell of a ride, ain't it?"

"You got that right, Skip. We'll standby on sixteen, give us a shout if we need to change course quickly."

"Will do, Long John. Island Time back to sixteen."

The decks of both boats were completely awash and the cockpit enclosures were doing a fantastic job of keeping the crew dry and warm, though they were taking a tremendous pounding. I just hoped a large wave wouldn't come across the deck and remove the whole damn thing. We were pitching wildly now as the waves were reaching heights I didn't think were even possible in the Sound. Breaking normal radio etiquette, Larry came back on the radio, not bothering to switch channels to a working channel from sixteen. He just announced with obvious delight in his voice...

"Calypso, the stacks are just in view, two hundred yards off the starboard bow at about one o'clock, do you copy?"

John responded affirmatively and we all breathed a sigh of relief, far too soon. Within seconds, a loud snap at the stern of the boat garnered all of our attention. We turned to see our inflatable dinghy, which had been resting comfortably suspended from the stern on stainless steel dinghy davits, hanging from its bow by only one davit. The line holding the stern to the port davit had separated. The dinghy was banging wildly against the stern of Calypso each time a giant wave ran under us. The dinghy outboard motor had been removed and was securely attached to the stern rail, but if we did nothing, the dinghy, which we absolutely needed to go cruising, would quickly be history. John assessed the problem and offered up.

"Cappy, we're gonna' lose her for sure if we don't get there and bring her in. She can't stand much more bangin' around. Hook a tether to my harness and I'll go get her."

"I'll go too, John. Essie, think you can steer her?"

"Only since I was about four, Cappy. I'll hold her nose into the waves while you help John pull the dink back onboard."

We both hooked a tether to our harnesses and opened a side curtain to the rear of the cockpit enclosure. The moment we stepped out onto the deck, it was apparent how much the enclosure had been shielding us from the weather. The chilly day coupled with a thirty-knot wind had a chill factor that felt close to freezing. The wind driven spray literally stung our faces and the entire deck was awash with every passing wave. We braced ourselves against the wind and waves as we crawled to the stern of the boat, actually less than ten feet. The broken line that had held the stern of the dinghy was flailing wildly and popped us both across the face as we inched out to secure it. John made several bold grabs for it, finally catching hold after what seemed like hours.

"Got her, Cappy. Now let's try and grab the dink."

Twice, John grabbed for the rubber handles on the rear of the dink. He would have to let go each time the rubber vessel swung out with the movement of Calypso or be drug overboard.

"Cappy, you're gonna' have to hold me while I grab it. Tie yourself to the stern rail over by the dinghy davit we need to secure to and then hold my belt. If I go overboard, just help me use my tether to climb back up on board."

"I don't know, John, that sounds pretty dangerous to me. If you fall overboard here, getting you back topsides would be next to impossible. You sure you want to do this? I mean, we could probably find another used dink somewhere if we had to."

The wind was so loud through the rigging that, with the noise of the crashing waves, we could barely yell loud enough to hear one another.

"We gotta' do this quick, Cappy or we ain't gonna' have no dinghy to get to shore with when we get where we're going. Now, just hold onto my tether. I'll be fine."

I double wrapped John's tether around my wrists. If he fell overboard, there's no doubt we would both be in the water. As he lunged, the pressure against my wrists felt like it was going to rip my hands off. I gave it everything I had as John increased his leaning off the boat. He was now suspended only by the tether and his feet, which barely touched the side of Calypso. He was leaning so far out I didn't believe I would be able to hold him.

"Alright, Cappy, I've got her, now pull me back in."

Now, I knew my hands were going to leave my arms. I strained till there was nothing left in my back or arms to give. I could see my hands turning blue. I thought I was going to pass out from the pain.

"Alright, Cappy, we got her. She should at least make it

into port. You all right?"

"I don't know, John. How do my hands look?"

"I'd say it's going to be a six pack night for you, Cappy.

Silver Lake - The anchorage at Ocracoke Island "Heaven"

Let's get back in the cockpit 'fore another big wave comes through."

As we entered the enclosure, Essie, in complete control of Calypso, gave her a sharp turn away from the wind and then eased her off as the sails filled and we began driving towards the stacks.

"You fellas, just sit back. I'll get her in to Silver Lake."

"Can you still see Island Time?" I asked her.

"Nope, but I can see the stacks and I guess I've run this channel a couple hundred times over the years. We'll be fine."

And we were. She handled Calypso like a daysailer, making every marker perfectly and sheeting in the sails to get the maximum performance for each angle we took to the wind as she followed the Big Foot Channel into Silver Lake. Impressed? Yes, in a big way. As the blood began to come back into my hands, it brought a pretty sizable dose of pain with it. I could tell from the sensations that I suffered no permanent damage, but I had enough rope burns and abrasions to go around for all of Ocracoke Island. I was ready to be there.

Chapter Three

As we pulled into Silver Lake, past the Coast Guard station and the ferry docks, I could feel my spirits starting to soar. This had always been one of my favorite places. The best way to describe Ocracoke is to say it's Key West forty years ago. The town is basically built in a half-moon shape around Silver Lake. Silver Lake is a very large, totally protected anchorage that has welcomed sailors for several hundred years. It has a beautiful old lighthouse on the ocean side which is visible from anywhere in the anchorage, day or night. Many times we had anchored in Silver Lake, but this time we decided to stay at the Anchorage Marina. This quaint dock has a small but attractive hotel overlooking the harbor and about thirty boat slips that are used by transient boaters visiting the island. My favorite feature of the Anchorage is the large gazebo built out over the water at the end of the pier where the boat slips are. If you're staying there, Sue, who runs the place, will let you use the gazebo as a private platform for all kinds of wonderful parties. I was hoping for such an impromptu gathering this evening. God knows, it would take more than a beer to make me forget the burning on my wrists. Larry and Linda Jo were waiting at the dock to take our lines.

"Why did you guys turn around out there? We looked back and one minute you were right behind us and the next you were almost out of sight. Have a problem?"

"We were playing save the dinghy. We won, but there were some players injured."

I held out my rope-burned wrists for evidence. Linda Jo offered, "I've got some medicated salve for burns on the boat. I'll get you some and we'll wrap those wrists overnight. You'll be a lot better by morning. I don't think they look bad enough to blister. You will be in some pain tonight though."

"Well, I have the cure for that. Let's go to the Jolly Roger and get a burger and beer. Then, we can clean up and let the festivities begin."

No one protested the plan, so we finished securing Calypso and the five of us headed on foot to the little waterfront bar and grill. The Jolly Roger, like almost every place on the island, had a pirate theme. This was to take advantage of the notoriety of Ocracoke's most famous citizen, Edward Teach, better known to the world as Blackbeard. Blackbeard had considered Ocracoke and Teach's Hole, a secluded anchorage, his base of operations for about a two year period, up till his capture and beheading at the Island by government authorized troops from Virginia. He was a local hero, even at that time, sharing his booty with local residents who served aboard his ship, the Queen Anne's Revenge. The ship, famous for it's owner and storied history of looting ships off the coast, had recently been found in eighteen feet of water about a mile outside of Beaufort Inlet, not too far from Ocracoke. This had started a tremendous amount of publicity for the entire area and it's notorious past. Local governments and merchants immediately saw a possible boon to the economy and began pushing the Blackbeard ties to the area. Whatever the reasons for its name, the Jolly Roger was a great place to spend an hour or an evening. We had all done both many times.

The Jolly Roger was hopping this evening. As we commandeered a large picnic table on the porch which sat out over the water on pilings, a voice called from another table.

"Ahoy there, Calypso and Island Time, this is Seeker calling."

That could be none other than Lawyer Larry, our friend from back in New Bern and a fellow sailor. He had a smaller but elegant twenty-eight footer and had accompanied us on many cruises. He was there with his steady girl, Lisa, who we all called Sprout because of her diminutive size. Once you got to know her, her fiery personality and go for it attitude made her seem a lot larger in stature. It was apparent; they had been toasting the Island all afternoon.

"Permission to join the fleet, Admiral," Larry offered up." Our group all enjoyed his quick wit though it often was a little too X-rated for some tastes.

"Permission, granted. Grab yourselves a chair. How long have you been over here? We didn't see Seeker as we pulled in."

"We're over at the State Docks. You know me, not one to waste money, at least at a marina. Now here, well that's a different story. That's if you consider this wasting money."

Everyone voiced their mutual agreement that this was money well spent.

"How long you here for, Lawyer Larry?"

"We would have already been on the way home, probably just about there by now if this gale hadn't blown in. You guys sailed in right through it, didn't you? How was it?"

John Silver answered in his typical manner, which I had begun to recognize as understated alarmism. Basically, this means that he would downplay a situation while giving just enough exaggerated details of some sort of crisis to intrigue one's interest.

"It was basically a nice ride, couldn't ask for better winds. Don't think Les is going to require hospitalization, but, we'll keep a close watch on him for circulation problems in his hands. Wouldn't want gangrene to set in, might lose his hands if that were the case. But, I think we're all right, none the worse for the sorta' conditions we were in. I'm not looking for a medal or anything. Saved lots of folks fore' this."

I thought to myself, nice going, John. That should give you enough lead-ins for the whole evening's story telling period. Larry could hardly contain himself.

"Jesus, Les, what the hell happened out there? Let me see your hands."

"Well, they're already bandaged up now. But, I'll let you know immediately if they have to run me to the mainland hospital or if it looks like I'm going to lose them, both. Say, how do you get a Life-Flight chopper out here?"

Larry repeated his question, hoping for a more straightforward answer, I'm sure.

"What on Earth happened out there?"

"John Silver can certainly tell it better than me. I mean, I was in so much agony that I can't even clearly recall all the details. I'll let John tell you. Essie, you want a drink, darlin'? Beer, wine cooler?"

"Make it a pina-collada."

She looked at the waitress as she continued.

"And keep the blender warm, I'll be needing more than one, or two."

Photo by David C. Eanes

Lawyer Larry (Larry Economos) - Unique beyond words

still blowing hard outside. It felt marvelous to be in such a unique place with good friends, both new and old. The deck we were on was basically an open one that had been enclosed with thin plastic sheeting, the kind that a lot of folks use down south as a cheap form of storm windows. It was almost like the window on a convertible top. Out in the harbor, the anchor lights from a dozen or so sailboats looked like dancing white lights on a Christmas tree while the lighthouse, with its continuously circling beam, was the Angel on the top branch. With such a fabulous view, it was no wonder that so many folks had visited Ocracoke and decided to stay and open a little restaurant or gift shop. For that reason, the place was growing. I wished it could be frozen in time, just as it was right now. Not another store or home or four wheel drive fishing vehicle with New Jersey plates. Why can't something so perfect just stay as it is? And while I was so deep in thought, another crew came trundling in from the dark windy night. It was Dennis and Joan off Kestrel, and with them was something that I knew would make this evening special. Dennis had brought his old Martin guitar. He and Joan both sang wonderfully with a bent towards the country classics. I loved to hear them. Dennis would finger-pick and sing harmony to Joan who had a fantastic voice, much like a Patsy Cline or Loretta Lynn. Chairs from all over the deck were pulled into a circle and an impromptu concert began. Though he preferred to sing country, Dennis could play just about anything anybody could hum and before long, the Aneheiser Busch choir was in full swing. For about three hours, songs that I could barely remember, to all the Jimmy B. sailing classics filled the deck at the Jolly Roger. At about one A.M., Larry stood up and announced.

"Friends, it's drawing near to that time of evening when we must retire to our individual ships and reward our crews for their devoted labor on this voyage."

He winked at Sprout as he made that section of his statement. She responded in kind and we all knew where this was going. He continued.

"And so, in the time honored tradition of all of us who have traversed the wide and always unpredictable oceans in our small yet magnificent vessels, I hereby request that we end this splendid evening with the National Anthem."

Everyone cheered as Dennis began to play and then the entire assemblage broke into the only song that could truly be called that, Magaritaville. It was sung with great enthusiasm and volume with the final chorus repeated at least two times more than the original called for. After that, everyone hugged everyone else's woman and vice versa while relating how much they all loved each other. Then, we broke into our own little entourages and departed back to our respective boats. What a wonderful evening. This is what my soul had been needing. I didn't know how I would ever be able to sustain this voyage with so little money, but for now, all was right with my world.

Calypso was tied up at the end of the longest pier, against the far end of the gazebo. As we walked towards her, Lawyer Larry and Lisa accompanied us. He was not three sheets into the wind, but perhaps two and two thirds sheets. We bade them goodnight and stepped aboard. As we turned to see them off, Larry, dancing to tunes that only he was hearing, danced right off the pier into the quite cold October water.

We all ran over to the spot where he had gone over, and the deck was a full five feet above the water level. We fully expected to have to jump in after him. But, as we looked down, he popped up like a cork, holding his eyeglasses in one hand and his beer in the other. He smiled as he said to us...

"Full gainer with a one and half twist, can I get a nine five for that one?"

While laughing to gut splitting proportions, we managed to pull him back on the deck and this time we escorted him back to Seeker and tucked him in. What a character, I thought out loud.

The aft stateroom berth felt like a suite at a five star hotel. My aching back and wrists needed some well-deserved rest. I laid back, pulled the comforter up over me and thought back over the wonderful times I had on the water. I had grown up on the James River in Newport News, Virginia and had a homemade sailboat by the time I was ten. Later, my father, who was a skilled craftsman, helped me build a Penguin. Actually, I held the light while he worked and I painted her. She was beautiful and did as much for creating the desire to sail in me as anything else in my life. She carried me up and down the river, in safety and with a good turn of speed. Every sailor understands that a good dinghy sailor makes a good big boat sailor. A dinghy is far trickier and if you make a mistake, she'll dump your butt in the water. A big boat does everything slower and with ten times the stability. Whatever the reason as to how I got infected with the sailing-gypsy bug, I had it since I was very young. I thought back to my first decent sized sailboat, a twenty-three footer that I taught my kids how to sail in. They like to say that I was Captain Bligh when they were on her with me, that I was continually barking orders and complaining. I never realized this till they told me, which was several years after the fact. They said I had made sailing a very nerve racking experience for them. Later, when they were older and I had another, larger boat, I made up my mind that from then on out, no matter what was happening on board, as long as it wasn't life threatening, I wouldn't fuss. I have lived by that rule every since and generally find that everyone is happier and nothing dire has occurred as a result. I tell this story to young and first time sailors. Don't panic and don't scream at everyone because you're scared or nervous. Just take your time and think about what you are doing and you'll find that is a better, more productive way to handle a boat. Thinking about the good times I had with my kids on board and some of the adventures we had shared, distracted me from my aching body and let me fall quickly into a deep sleep.

The sun, pouring in through the hatch over my head, brought me back to the real world. My hands didn't ache quite so intensely though my back was still a little stiff. It was apparent that sitting at a desk in an cubicle, staring at a computer screen for eight hours a day for years, was not the appropriate training for life onboard a cruising sailboat. I slipped on my jeans and stepped into the cockpit, to be greeted by my crew as well as Larry, Linda Jo, Lawyer Larry and Sprout. Essie smiled warmly and asked me,

"Pancakes and blueberry syrup, Cappy? And, I've got some coffee with Irish Creme in it, or how about a Bloody Mary to trim your sails this morning?"

"It all sounds good. Let's start with the pancakes and coffee."

"Coming up, Cappy."

I greeted my accomplices from the previous evening.

"Good morning to all of you. Trust you all slept the sleep of the dead as I did."

Lawyer Larry looked a little haggard, but Lisa was smiling brightly.

"Well, Les" Larry started.

"I'm not a hundred percent yet, but this Bloody Mary is bringing me around. When are you guys planning on heading out? Going to stay here a few more days?"

"No, I don't think so. I love Ocracoke. It's one of the all time great places. But, there are so many others I haven't seen. I want to get started checking them out. How about you? What's your agenda? Or is there one?"

"Unfortunately, my land-lines are made of stainless steel. I've got court on Wednesday, so I'll be heading back today. Island Time said they were going to tag along with us. So, after breakfast, we'll all be getting underway back to New Bern. It ain't going south to the Bahamas for the winter, like some folks we know are doing, but New Bern is a great place."

"You're right, it is and it will always be home for me. But, I want to ride the coconut express, just once. I think we'll tag along with you guys till we get to Adam's Creek and then we'll head towards Beaufort Inlet while you keep on going up-river."

"Man, wish I could go with you."

Larry and Linda Jo and the rest of the breakfast crew nodded their heads in agreement.

"Well, I guess we better top off our fuel and water and then, we're ready. Give us an hour."

"That'll be just about right for all of us. Good luck and Godspeed, Calypso."

All our friends chimed in together.

"Aye, Aye, Calypso, Godspeed!"

We all hugged and then everyone set about readying for the next step in our respective journeys.

We readied Calypso quickly; double securing the dinghy this time and giving everything on deck a strong visual inspection. We had just witnessed how much trouble a frayed line could cause and none of us wished for a repeat performance. John called out from the nav station below.

"Cappy, come take a listen to the weather channel."

I stepped below and he turned up the volume.

"Low pressure is continuing to build and the probability for a nor'easter continues to increase later in the week. Mariners headed offshore in the mid-Atlantic region should monitor this weather pattern closely."

"Well, John. We'll do exactly that. Sometimes, I've heard, the best sailing when you're going south is right behind a nor'easter. But, you're right, I don't want to do anything risky. We don't have to hurry anywhere, do we?"

"I sure as hell don't, Cappy. We'll just keep a sharp weather-eye and poke along south. As far as I'm concerned, we're ready to head out."

"Let's give the other boats a shout on the radio and then we'll cast off our lines."

"Aye, aye, Cappy."

Within minutes, our little fleet was underway. Dennis and Joan stood under the gazebo and waved to us as we departed. This was becoming a quite common experience, seeing us off. I looked back at the lovely village as we slipped out of Silver Lake and back into the Pamlico Sound. There was still a good strong breeze blowing, though it had turned till it was blowing out of the northeast. When headed towards Ocracoke, that is the worst wind direction possible, but when returning, it gave us a good strong wind on our stern though we had some nice rollers to go along with it. I never minded some movement to the boat when she was sailing. I rather enjoyed it, as long as it had a rhythm and the boat wasn't pounding dramatically. Island Time and Seeker were both alongside for at least part of our journey. Island Time, at thirty thousand pounds was enjoying the strong conditions and riding easily, as was Calypso. We displaced only nineteen thousand pounds, but that was still a right smart number for a thirty-nine footer. Seeker, on the other hand, was only twenty-eight foot in length and weighed in at sixty-eight hundred pounds. She was strong and sailed well, but these conditions were still much more of a test to her than to us. I could see Lawyer Larry, smiling as he worked the wheel, playing each wave as a porpoise might a breaking wave in the surf. These were good friends, and I wish I could have brought the entire fleet south with us. We crossed the Pamlico and entered the mouth of the Neuse in just under four hours. Marker NR appeared to our port and the conditions started to moderate a little. We sailed fairly tight together, where we could joke with the other skippers and crew with our voices alone. No need for the radio. As we came upon Neuse Marker number seven, Oriental was back on our starboard and we knew the time for separation was at hand. We raised a toast to the other boats who followed in kind and within a few minutes, the fleet was no more. The two boats that were carrying our friends back to our homeport sailed on without us as we turned south, towards Beaufort and the Atlantic Ocean.

"Cappy" and Captain Larry Basden on Island Time

Chapter Four

Though I had been down Adam's Creek many times, this trip was different. As we took a separate course from Island Time and Seeker, it finally seemed like we were on our own and heading towards adventure. Adam's Creek is mainly a man-made canal, much like the Dismal Swamp Canal in southern Virginia. It enabled boats up to about seven feet in draft to stay inshore on their way south. With Cape Hatteras, the Graveyard of the Atlantic just offshore in this area, it certainly allowed a lot more folks to go south for the winter. Most would be quite nervous to stay offshore in this area. I know I would. As we neared the middle of the ten mile inland stretch to Beaufort, we passed Seagate Marina. I had kept a previous boat there for a couple of years and met some quite interesting characters. The most notable of these was Edna Burke.

I had just purchased a lovely thirty foot Pearson Coaster, a vintage (1967) sloop with gracious lines and tremendous sailing characteristics. She had been on the hard for six months as the young man I had hired to paint her had led me down a primrose path throughout the entire process. He told me it would take a month to paint and that he wanted a fifty percent deposit, or twenty five hundred bucks up front. The rest would be due when he finished. After five months of pleading, he hadn't touched the boat. I had found out that this was his normal modus operandi and that each of the four previous suckers, er boat owner's had the same problem with him. He apparently spent the deposit to keep his creditors off the doorstep and then he had no interest in doing the work since he would basically get half of what the job was worth and he would have to pay for the paint, help, etc. with that. About the fifth month, now understanding the situation, I told him that I was taking off the next morning and going to the Sheriff's Office. He asked me,

"You're going to sue me, aren't you?"

To which, I gleefully replied.

"Absolutely not! A judgement against somebody with credit like yours isn't worth the time of day. I'm going to go swear out a warrant against you for fraud and obtaining property through false pretenses. If I can't get the work done or my money back, I will at least have the satisfaction of seeing you in jail. You'd probably be interested to know that several of your other customers have indicated to me that they would be very happy to testify in court against you. I'm betting you can get a couple of years in the State Pen for this. Sounds like fun, don't it?"

The sweat began to pour from under his dirty ball cap and for the first time in half a year, I could discern a real concern for doing a good job for me on his face.

"Give me two weeks and I promise you she'll be done, just two weeks, I'll drop everything and get right on it."

"Well, you do understand that I'm not joking about this, two weeks and that's it."

"It will be ready."

And ready it was. He had completed a beautiful Awlgrip paint job. She looked new. It took me almost a year however, to caulk everything on the boat he had removed to paint her. He put it all back on without any caulk in an effort to make the problem (me) go away. I had learned another valuable boating lesson that I still use today. I don't hire anyone to do anything on a boat for me unless there is absolutely no other way. Generally there is always another sailor at the marina who knows how to accomplish the task and will gladly lead me through it as long as I am always willing to reciprocate when they have a problem. This has turned out to be a Godsend. If the isolated problem arises that no one can help me with and I am forced to go to a marine 'professional' and God, I use that word loosely here, I get a detailed proposal in writing that includes time and money. The guys working at most of the boatyards, in our area at least, make folks like Edward Teach seem like Sunday School teachers. During this same time, a very difficult learning period for me, I had hired an engine 'expert' to hook up the throttle connection to my old Atomic Four gas engine. It was just laying beside the engine and appeared to need nothing much more than a cotter pin to be fixed. I also asked him to change the oil and plugs and make sure she was running properly. I called him up the next week as I was driving to New Bern. He indicated all the work was done but he wanted to meet me at a local restaurant downtown since he was already in that area and didn't want to drive back out to the marina. I agreed, happy that my boat was finally ready to move out of this den of pirates. We shook hands and exchanged pleasantries. I then asked the dreaded question,

"what do I owe you?"

Without batting an eye, he replied,

"Five hundred and forty five bucks! I had to have a part machined out of brass to secure the throttle since these old British engines don't have parts around here. I'll get the oil and plugs tomorrow."

I was too flabbergasted to even protest. With trembling hands, I wrote the check and left. I know all the blood had left my face. I'm sure I looked like a man who had just received the news from his doctor that he had a week to get his affairs in order. As I walked out, he yelled out to me,

"Hey, I'll get the oil and plugs and then send you a bill!"

I had never even realized that the engine was an American made mainstay of the boating industry for over thirty years and he had referred to it as British. That would have given me some insight into his knowledge base.

The next week, I got another bill from him for forty five dollars for the oil change and plugs. I thought to myself, "yeah, when Hell freezes over he'll get this."

So, that brings me back to my story. I had asked my friend Henry Heath to accompany me on my maiden voyage with BeginAgin as I took her from the boatyard, down the Neuse, through Adam's Creek, all the way to Wilmington, North Carolina where her homeport would be. Henry had done very little sailing at that time and his better half, Brenda, cautioned him about burial at sea. I don't know why she had so little faith in me. We were sailing along wonderfully with a brisk northerly breeze. As we neared the ferry crossing at Minnesott Beach, the skies began to darken and I could hear the faint rumblings of thunder coming up on us from the stern. I decided to check the weather channel on my VHF. I was more than a little alarmed by the announcement that was being repeatedly broadcast.

"Notice to mariners, there is a line of severe thunderstorms moving due east across the state at thirty miles and hour. There is the possibility of severe lightning, hail and high winds. All boaters should seek shelter to avoid this storm immediately. The area of highest probability is in a line between Havelock and Oriental, North Carolina."

Henry asked me,

"and where are we right now?"

"Our position could best be described as in a line between Havelock and Oriental, North Carolina."

I could see the worry in his eyes.

"That's bad, isn't it?"

I did my best John Wayne impression.

"Don't you worry there, soldier, we'll be just fine."

The storm was now bearing down quickly on us. There was very severe lightning and high winds. We immediately lowered and secured the mainsail. I left up the small working jib and started the newly rejuvenated Atomic Four engine. She started beautifully and I thought to myself,

"Five hundred bucks was a lot, but you just can't beat knowing that your motor is there when you really need it."

Within five minutes, the engine sputtered and died, completely dead. Dead. I thought to myself,

"It's probably no use to just sit here and cry right now. It might scare Henry and there's always plenty of time to do it later, in private, over a beer. Yeah, that's what I'll do."

I had never gone down Adam's Creek before. It was detailed fairly well on the map I had. So, with just the headsail alone, coupled with the strong winds the thunderstorm had generated, we continued down river towards Adam's Creek. It was dark by the time we arrived at the mouth of the creek. With no motor and now a dying wind, we inched along, following marker after marker. If I had known in advance what a winding, shallow, convoluted trail I was following, I probably would have just gone to Oriental for the night and anchored. But, ignorance must be the father of all exploration. We continued on. Finally, I had my first experience with a range marker. These are white markers, unlike the red and green channel markers that normally mark rivers and the intracoastal waterway (ICW) that we were on. Range markers, in a nutshell, consist of two white lights, blinking at different timed intervals. For example, one may blink every three seconds and the other every eight, or even be permanently on. The theory is, you line up one directly under the other and you will be in the channel. I have found in subsequent years that this really does work quite nicely. However, you shouldn't experiment in the fashion we were doing this particular evening. Eventually, I continued to follow the rear white light, not knowing how in the Hell the system was supposed to work. I found out the hard way that the rear marker was in approximately two feet of water. We begin to touch bottom. It was extremely calm by this time. The trees on either side of Adam's Creek were blocking what little wind there was. I didn't have a good grasp on where to go and I was too damn tired to keep going. I had a solution.

"I'm going to throw out the anchor and get some rest. The tide will come in around four AM and we'll get about a foot more water. We can ease back out into the channel then."

I was guessing that the white light was not the correct one to be following and that moving towards a distant green one had to be the way to go. I collapsed into my bunk as did Henry. About four AM, as predicted, I could feel the hull start to bounce a little on the bottom indicating we were just barely floating again. I woke up, still exhausted but knowing we needed to make good our escape.

"I'll raise the jib and we can ghost along to the main channel."

I went forward and raised the jib. The wind was about one knot and we started to just barely eke out towards the green light. A fairly dense fog was covering the creek making visibility somewhat difficult. It would take a spotlight to find our markers. The depth finder started to indicate that we were headed in the correct direction. I plugged our high beam, handheld spotlight in and shined it towards the reflective marker. The depth kept increasing, five feet, six feet, seven, eight, ten, voila! We were in the channel again. It was just about that very moment when we were centered in the channel, under minimal sail power alone, just ghosting along, that the mind-numbing blare of a fog horn pierced the early morning fog and lifted me into the air, completely off my butt. I knew the sound and realized it wasn't far off. My crew didn't know what the sound indicated, but my surprise flight had certainly not gone unnoticed by him.

"What the hell was that?"
I had a lot of help in answering his question. No sooner had the words left his mouth than a bright spotlight came out of nowhere and illuminated our cockpit.

"Tug pushing a barge, he's coming right at us and he won't be able to stop or go around us in this tight channel. We've got to come about and get out of his way."

I turned the tiller hard over and with the extremely light air, we ghosted around, as if in slow motion. I shined our spotlight on our sail so that the tugboat skipper could see us. As close as he was, there was nothing he could do to avoid a collision if we couldn't get out of his way. I shined the light on his barge, or should I say barges as he was pushing two incredibly large fertilizer carriers in front of him. They were as tall out of the water as the spreaders on our mast, perhaps thirty feet or so. We continued to creep along as he churned quickly towards us. The speed of a tugboat with barges is very deceiving and will generally catch most smaller sailboats when they are wide open. In the wind we were working with, it was definitely a tortoise and the hare situation. I think we both aged several years over the two minute period. As the barges passed within ten feet of our stern, the bow wave pushed us from behind as if we were surfing. Within a minute, they were past and all was dark and still. In the distance, the rumble of the tug's diesel sounded like a freight train going over a mountain. It was a pretty frightening occurrence. I can remember it clearly, ten years later. I looked over at Henry.

"So, how are you this morning? Ready for some coffee?"

He was visibly shaken.

"I think I need a beer."

"At five AM?"

"You're right, I need whiskey."

Henry and Brenda Heath

I don't remember whether or not he actually started the morning off with a shot, but things eventually settled down and the sun came up. We moved like a snail down Adam's Creek till the wind became completely on our nose and we could make no more progress in the appropriate direction to reach our destination. We dropped the anchor again and I looked in the Coastal North Carolina Cruising Guide to try and find the closest place to try and make. It was now about lunchtime. I saw that Seagate Marina was just about three miles further down Adam's Creek. I tried to raise them on channel sixteen numerous times with no luck. I was running out of ideas and the one possible solution was not very palatable. The Coast Guard no longer responded to calls of this nature. They had become basically an answering service for tow companies. A three mile tow from a service out of Oriental or Beaufort would cost around three hundred bucks. I had tow insurance but I sure didn't want to use it for something as trivial as this. In theory, we could wait for the wind to come back and in a favorable direction to sail to Seagate. That could take anywhere from the next five minutes to sometime next week, knowing the fickleness of the wind. I decided to try one last time for Seagate Marina.

"Seagate Marina, Seagate Marina, this is BeginAgin calling."

After four or five tries a response came back.

"BeginAgin, this is the sailing vessel Sashay calling, switch to channel sixty-eight."

The voice was that of a woman. I figured she must be the wife of a live-aboard skipper. Delighted at finally raising the possibility of a solution to our dilemma, I quickly switched channels.

"Go ahead Sashay, this is BeginAgin."

"Yes, BeginAgin, where the hell are you and what's the problem. They don't monitor the radio here like they should sometimes."

"Well, we're about three miles north of you on Adam's Creek in a thirty foot sailboat. Motor's D.O.A. and we need to get a tow to Seagate. Anybody there who might tow us?"

"Nobody, but me. I'll come and get you. Just stand by on sixteen and I'll be there in about fifteen minutes. Sashay back to sixteen."

I didn't really understand what she meant by "I'll come and get you" but she sounded like she knew what she was talking about. I was expecting someone in a powerboat, probably a seventeen foot Boston Whaler to appear any minute. What appeared was a little surprising. I could hear the noise of a small outboard coming our way. Then, around the bend in front of us appeared a ten foot inflatable dinghy. Standing upright in the center of it, was a person wearing tan shorts with a matching safari shirt, sleeves rolled up, holding onto a rope attached to the bow with one hand and the other clamped onto a PVC handle extension connected to the outboard motor. It was a pretty unusual sight. As the dinghy got closer, I could see that the person steering this craft was a woman, about fifty five, maybe sixty years old, a short cropped mop of gray hair over a face carved out of stone with deep blue eyes offering the only relief from her weathered features. She had the stance and muscular physique of a thin man and steered the dinghy with confidence that only comes from many years of performing a task. She came up behind us and asked,

"you folks, BeginAgin?"

"That's us. You with Sashay?"

"Sure am. I'm Edna, Edna Burke. Tell you what I think we're gonna' have to do here. My little dink probably won't tow you very well, so I'm gonna get behind you and just nuzzle my bow against you and push you to the marina."

"You think it will push us? We're pretty heavy."

"I know it will. You just steer and I'll ease up when you need to turn into the marina."

And so I met Edna. She pushed us into a slip at the marina. After getting the boat secured, she had us aboard her twenty-eight foot British Channel Cutter. Turns out, she was a widow who had traveled with her husband, Burt, all over the Caribbean for a number of years. He died of heart problems a couple years prior to our meeting. She continued to live aboard after his death as she just loved the sea and boats. She had acquired her

Master's License along the way and did yacht deliveries and charters to pick up a little extra money. She loved to argue with anyone who was willing and made fast friends and hard enemies. Her heart was just as good as gold, but she had to be one of the most contrary women God ever put on the planet. I just generally let her have her say and then did just as I was going to do without her input. She certainly did know boats and sailing. I hired her to re-rig the running lines on my boat and a number of other projects, even putting in a new gas tank. Everything she did was done perfectly and for a reasonable amount of money, something I hadn't experienced previously in my boat dealings. She was the one who discovered that the plugs and oil had not been changed in the engine as Mr. Marine Mechanic had asserted. What a lying bastard he was. She helped me tune the motor and when it and the other jobs she was doing had been completed, I was forced with the decision of whether to continue on to Wilmington or stay at Seagate. I opted to remain where I was, and thus, a fast friendship was born. I would come down on Friday evenings after work. A group of us would all go into Beaufort to a small restaurant and bar we loved and listen to music and dance all evening. For all her disdain of things female, my Gawd, she wouldn't even shave her legs, Edna loved to shake a leg and we generally would share a few dances while we were there. Some of the other guys told me they had assumed she must be a dyke, which was definitely not the case. We never had anything romantic between us, but I could certainly tell that she would love to have another man in her life. I always loved feminine women. I require lots of affection and wanted desperately to lavish it on a woman who caught my fascination and my eye. I had remained faithful to my wife for over twenty eight years, even though the last dozen or so had been with the lifestyle of a priest. I knew, if there was ever going to be another woman in my life, it would be a torrid affair. Edna had the boating qualifications I needed in a woman, but she just didn't want to work at things like makeup or being female. I don't want to underestimate the value of a woman loving sailboats and living on board one. These women are very rare and should be cherished. Very few women can deal with the limited space for 'stuff' that exists on a boat. Any yacht broker will tell you that the largest single factor in buying or selling a sailboat is marital status. Get divorced, buy a boat. Get married, sell a boat. Some women can tolerate it in little doses, especially if the man won't make it 'tilt' over. I've seen countless numbers of married men, at their boat, alone. Their wife won't come down any longer and they finally get completely discouraged and sell their dream. I had vowed that would never happen to me again. My wife had gotten seasick standing on the floating dock next to the boat. That is no lie. And, she considered it to be a big imposition on her to go sailing with me two weekends a year. Oh, how I longed for her to want to be on the boat with me, anchored in a small cove, watching the sun go down. That was never going to happen now. We were both going to be happier for my running away. Eventually, I grew tired of the long motoring required to get to sailing waters from Seagate, approximately an hour either way up or down Adam's Creek and I moved the boat to New Bern. There, I could be sailing within five minutes. After that, I saw Edna occasionally in Beaufort or talked to her on the VHF, but we drifted apart and thus ended many wonderful cruises. I truly hoped she would find a guy salty enough to see her as beautiful. These thoughts all ran through my mind as we passed the entrance to Seagate. We didn't stop.

By the time we reached the Newport River and could see

the high-rise bridge separating Beaufort from Morehead City, it was late in the afternoon. John Silver had the wheel, I was laid back enjoying the view and Essie was down below throwing together some salsa and chips. We were all getting a little hungry and anxious to be anchored in Taylor's Creek. Finally, we made the hard port turn near the Beaufort Inlet and picked us out a nice anchorage, directly across Taylor's Creek from downtown Beaufort. The creek was filled almost to capacity with 'snowbirds'. That is the name used to describe sailor's that head south in the winter and north in the summer. The larger boats were being moved by professional, hired delivery skippers, and the smaller ones were generally folks just like us, making there own way south. The large number and variety of boats made Beaufort a sailor's visual smorgasbord.

Chapter Five

Beaufort is a working seaport. It's the preeminent stop for sailor's heading north and south on the eastern seaboard. It offers a good all weather inlet, and all the facilities and watering holes one could ask for. It had been a working, fishing, and shrimping town till recent years. More recently, tourists and yachtsman had fallen victim to her charms and now dominated the landscape with beautiful yachts of every description and an onslaught of tourism. All of the old fish-houses were now boutiques and restaurants. There were a number of salty bars and nightclubs offering a wide array of musical styles and atmospheres. I particularly loved seeing all the visiting sailboats and meeting folks who had thrown away their landlines and were going for it. I always envied them. Now, I was them. We took the dinghy and headed into the waterfront to stretch our legs a bit. As we got to the main boardwalk, we noticed a crowd in front of the Docksider listening to a band. It turned out to be a group that I enjoyed immensely, who did all of Buffett's stuff plus a lot of old classic rock. I knew where I would be spending the evening. The Docksider is one of the best known watering holes in Beaufort. It's right on the boardwalk and when the weather is nice, bands play out on the deck overlooking the harbor. If the band's any good, the boardwalk running in front will fill to capacity with folks listening to the music. This evening was no exception. John Silver had drug out that ridiculous eye patch and bandana again, but Essie, all I can say is Amen, brother. She had donned a form fitting summer dress, low cut front and back, and snug around the waist. A little dab of makeup here and there, and she was the cream of the crop this evening. She stood by the small area in front of the band where a few people would always be dancing, and started to move to the music. It wasn't long before she was getting enough taps on the shoulder from the young men in the crowd to practically form a line. She made her selection and took to the floor. With her hands over her head, clapping to the beat of the music and her shapely hips gyrating to the music, she was quite spectacular. I thought to myself, "the other women might as well take a seat, Essie has stolen the show."

The real "Essie" Susanne Pendleton

The band decided it was time to take a break. Essie came over and sat down with me while John Silver made the rounds of the bar inside, hitting on every woman that would give him the time of day. I leaned back in my chair, looked out over the anchor lights on the mast tops of all the sailboats and thought to myself, "I'm finally starting to relax. I can feel the tension leaving my body. Maybe, just this once in my life I've made the right decision. What I had been needing all along was to simplify my life."

Let me pause in my tale here for just a moment. Isn't it always the case that just when you think things seem to be working out, you just don't see the train coming straight at you? Here I was, happy with my mid-life crisis management. I was smug, thinking I had it all figured out. It's exactly like that moment in a Roadrunner cartoon when old Willy Coyote thinks the hole he has cut in the bridge under the Roadrunner is going to drop his fleet footed arch-rival to a terrible, rock filled valley below, when all of a sudden, the entire bridge falls and only the hole remains with the Roadrunner on it. Willey Coyote takes the fall himself. So, what I'm getting at here is, I've just finished sawing the hole in the bridge and I'm waiting for the Roadrunner to plummet. Now, where was I? Oh yes, I remember now.

By now, the evening was spectacular, I'd had about five beers, two beyond my limit. The music had me in the mood and Essie, God she was beautiful, was sitting right across from me, also supremely happy with the evening. I wanted to take her back to Calypso and fornicate with her for at least an hour. When you're close to fifty, you have to be realistic with your dreams. We were small-talking when, out of the corner of my ear, I could hear the quiet, deep rumble of a large engine getting progressively louder. I turned to look in the direction of the noise and saw an immense amount of lights on the water coming up Taylor's Creek. At first, I thought it might be several boats coming in at once but quickly determined that the lights all belonged to the same vessel. Occasionally, small cruise ships, two hundred footers would dock in Beaufort and I assumed that must be the case. As the vessel came closer, one of the most magnificent private motor yachts I have ever seen came past the dock. It was at least a hundred and fifty footer. There were three levels of cabins above the deck. In back-lit, prominent, stainless steel letters near the top of the bridge, the name "Katz Meow" drew my attention. Now, Beaufort attracts the biggest and most impressive yachts in the world if they are cruising the East Coast. I know, I'd certainly seen my share of them. Why, even the king, no not Elvis, I'm talking Jimmy Buffett, brought his yacht in here whenever he was in the area. His new, ninety-foot Cheoy Lee motoryacht had been here just weeks prior to this. However, Katz Meow was near the top of the ladder of anything I'd ever seen. She was sparkling white and her pedigree and detailing shown through, even in just the reflected light against her silhouette. This was one impressive vessel. She was obviously expecting help from the dockhands that manage Beaufort's city docks. They were here alright, about two tables over from me and two six packs further into the evening. So, being a courteous yachtsman, and of course, wanting a little closer look, I grabbed John Silver and we went to the long finger pier at the far end of the dock in front of us and stood by to help with the lines. The vibration from the diesels, even though they were idling, was incredible. You could feel it in your stomach and even the pier seemed to vibrate. The skipper, certainly a professional captain hired by the owner, lined her up parallel to the pier and then, with the assistance of the bow thruster and two engines controlled independently of each other, he slid her right up against the pier. As she started to close, additional crew in spiffy white uniforms came to the side rail and dropped large round fenders over the side. I thought to myself, "the damn fenders are so large I couldn't even stow them onboard Calypso, I'd have to tow them. John and I took the offered lines and secured them to pilings fore and aft on the pier. We stood by and watched the crew lower a gangplank, just like a cruise ship. Several crew members came down and retied the lines we had secured, obviously to obtain prettier knots. Wouldn't want anyone thinking they would satisfy with just being secured. The Captain, a gray haired, sparkly toothed excerpt from a GQ add, stepped briskly to the dock, each move looking like a pose for a photo shoot, and thanked John and I for our assistance. He then made a fatal error. He offered to us,

"Gentlemen, once we are docked and secured, feel free to come to my quarters and accept a nightcap for your kind hospitality and assistance."

A professional skipper, huh? He shoulda' known better than that. The only one whose eyes had gotten bigger than mine were John Silver's who replied.

"We'll do just that, Skip. Uh, where are the Captain's Quarters?"

"Just ask the crewman stationed at the gangplank when you come aboard, he'll direct you. Give me about an hour."

"Will do, Skip."

Elated, we went back to our table at the Docksider, where Essie was seated, now with newly acquired male friends on either side of her.

"Boys, let me introduce you to Derick and, what did you say your name was again, there fella?"

"Smitty."

"Oh yeah, and my old friend, Smitty. Say hi, boys."

"Evening, boys. Can we have our seats back? Sorry to rush you."

The disapproval on their faces as they stood up and left was easily read. Essie was enjoying the attention.

"Guys, guys, why did you run off my old friends? We were just catching up on everything they've been doing since I met them, about ten minutes ago. So, how was the big boat?"

"Well, we'll let you judge for yourself. We've been invited aboard for a night cap in about an hour."

"You're shitting me!"

"You know I wouldn't do that."
"And I get to go too?"

"Wouldn't go without you."

"Alright! The next round is on me."

The hour passed quickly. We amused ourselves by watching the rather large amount of crew on Meow going about the tasks of setting up the lines, electricity, water; you name it, on such a large vessel. It was a lot of work, that was apparent. The Captain did no physical tasks on his own. He oversaw the operation and let nothing escape his keen eye. As they finished their tasks, the crew disappeared for a few minutes below and then about half of them came down the gangplank, dressed in civvies. Apparently, their employer did not want them going ashore flying his colors at non-official functions. They made their way over to the Docksider and began looking for a table on the already packed deck. Since it was time for us to go have our nightcap, we offered them our table. They were most appreciative. Essie eyed a couple of the flashy younger models and said,

"I'll come back for my seat in a while boys, save me a drink."

"You can count on it, missy."

We walked back down the pier and out to the gangplank leading up to the deck level on Meow. As promised, a uniformed crewmember stood watch at the top of the plank.

"Good evening folks, the Captain is expecting you. I'll have the Steward show you to his quarters. Thomas, come here please. Show these guests to Captain Arrington's please."

"Yes sir, please follow me."

We were all thinking the same thing. Jeez, was a life. We all tried to sneak a peak into the main salon as we passed, but as on almost every new mega-yacht, the windows were tinted so dark you could barely see a light on in the cabin. However, the door leading from the deck up the stairs to the salon was open slightly and I couldn't resist a quick look. I bent over just as I was properly centered in the doorframe, as if I had dropped something. As I slowly stood up and started to take my cursory look, my vision stopped knee-high on a killer pair of silk stocking encased legs. A voice from slightly above the knees said, I might add in a very sexy voice,

"Lose something?"

I continued my casual, I'm not impressed movement to an upright position. Directly in front of me stood one of the most beautiful women I'd ever seen. She was wearing a sheer white evening dress that showed about two thirds of her legs, starting somewhere halfway between her knees and Heaven. She was, I would say, best described as svelte and sophisticated but in a sexy way. Yeah, that's it in a nutshell.

"I, uh, dropped something."

"Didn't find it, did you?"

"Well, uh," She could see my hands were empty, think stupid, come up with something"

"I, er, uh, turns out I didn't drop it at all. It's here, still in my pocket." I reached deep into my pocket...nothing. I reached into the other side, finding a church-key I had been using on the boat earlier in the day. I pulled it out for her approval. She smiled sexily as she said,

"Oh, your beer opener, wouldn't want to lose that, would we? Never know when someone's going to offer you one without a pop-top."

By this time, I knew I had to be at least a little red in the face. I'm sure she was expecting me to ask if I could come in and check the TV for Hee Haw reruns. I smiled and turned to leave. Surprising me greatly, she added,

"When you get finished checking out the quite gay Captain's quarters, and oh yes, he'll be very disappointed that you and your friend brought a female with you, why don't you come up and let me show you the rest of my little ship?"

I was glad I had just taken a leak before we left the Dock-sider. Otherwise, I know I would have peed in my pants at that moment.

I composed myself quickly, and responded in the fashion of the worldly sort that I'm sure she expected of me.

"I'll be back in two shakes of a stick, Mam."

"You do that, Bubba. I'll be waiting right here."

Bubba...what the Hell did she mean by that? I made my way down the deck of the yacht to where the Steward was waiting impatiently for me.

"In here, Sir, the Captain has been waiting."

As I entered the Captain's quarters, it was hard not to be impressed with the room. Everything was either a rich teak, mahogany, or cherry. The fixtures were all highly polished brass and the furnishings were straight out Captain Nemo's private quarters. Of course, after seeing the boat from the outside, this really was no surprise. It's just that I had never been allowed on board one of these toys of the super rich before. The Captain, ever smiling, came to shake my hand.

"Ah, you made it. Boyd Arrington here, Captain Boyd my friends call me. And your name?"

"Les, Les Pendleton, and my friends call me Les or Cappy". I threw that in so as to not let myself be outranked.

"So, you have a vessel here in Beaufort?"

"Yes, a sloop, Calypso."

"Very good, Les. And she is....?"

"She is a.....Pearson, yes, a Pearson."

"Nice boats, how large a vessel?"

"A thirty-nine footer, a vintage model."

"Don't let my present situation fool you, Les. I've spent countless hours on small sailing vessels. Even lived on an old Irwin 38 Classic for years. Great boat. Whiskey? Scotch?"

"How about just a beer, Captain?"

"You got it. Steward" he yelled.

From just outside the door the Steward entered.

"Yes Sir?"

"Bring Captain Pendleton a beer, any preference, Les? and your crew here?"

"Well, a Corona would be wonderful I'm betting for all of us."

"You heard him, Steward."

"Yes, Sir. I'll be right back."

"So, gentlemen, miss…what do you think of Katz?"

I could not contain the fact that I was overly impressed. I had never been aboard anything quite this extravagant.

"Well, Captain Boyd, I'm certainly impressed. This is nicer than I thought it would be, and I thought it was going to be pretty damned spectacular. How many crew work on Katz?"

"There is a permanent crew of twelve, counting a maid, cook, steward, masseuse and the owner's personal assistant."

"And, who is the owner, if that's not confidential?"

"I'm sorry, that is highly confidential as you might expect. But, I can tell you that the owner is a very good person to work for. This is by far the best professional Skipper's position I've ever had. Essie, how would you and Captain Pendleton like the Steward to show you the deck layout? The cabins are private, of course, but the exterior decks are quite nice. I'll show John Silver here, the engine room as he indicated to me that he might like to see our power plants. How's that sound?"

"Just fine Captain Boyd. I'd love the tour as I'm sure Essie would."

As the Captain turned to direct the Steward to show us around topsides, I quickly looked at John and gave him an exaggerated limp wrist to help him avoid any surprise in his personal tour of the engine room. He looked at the Captain with a 'you're kidding?' look. I nodded in affirmation and then we left with the

Steward. I couldn't help but say to John as I left,

"John Silver, just look now, don't be touching the shaft."

Essie and I followed the Steward on a walk around the entire topsides of Katz Meow. For a yacht so large, it was hard to believe how immaculate everything was. All of the lines were neatly coiled. On deck behind the bridge, were two twenty-foot Boston Whalers that were used as the ship's launches. Alongside of these were four matching jet-skis. Still further back on the massive aft deck was the largest hot tub I had ever seen. It was the size of a small garden swimming pool. Steam was pouring off the water's surface and the lighting under the water made it appear a beautiful pale blue. Katz Meow was exactly that. As we rounded the for'deck and began our return on the starboard deck, a lighted entry into what appeared to be a ship's office was off to our side and directly under the yacht's bridge from where the boat would be controlled when under way. It was an intimate looking room with dark, richly polished teak walls, indirect lighting, and a large table that looked more like it should be in a board room in an office tower. On the wall were the words Leisey Corporation in burnished bronze letters, highlighted by an indirect spotlight. My curiosity overcame me. I asked the steward,

"Is that the ship's office? Pretty damned impressive."

He walked over to the door while Essie and I were still straining our necks to look in and closed the door firmly, never answering our question.

"Private quarters."

And, in a slightly exasperated tone, he added,

"Now, if you'll please stay right with me."

As much as I was enjoying the tour, I was even more enthused about the proposed tour that was waiting after this one was finished. After our deck walk, the Steward returned us to Captain Boyd's suite. There, laughing and enjoying a brandy was John Silver and Captain Boyd. I could only assume that everything in the engine room had ended on a happy note. The Captain asked us how we enjoyed the tour and then said he would love to come visit us on Calypso before they headed out the next afternoon. I readily agreed to a reciprocal tour at his convenience. He personally walked us to the ship's gangplank and I was ready to assume that the beautiful woman who teased me earlier was doing just that. No sooner had I put a foot on the plank, then I heard her say to Captain Boyd.

"Captain, please have the visiting Captain escort his crew back to his ship and then return to the salon."

There was no surprise on Captain Boyd's face. In fact, I thought I could ascertain a 'knowing' smirk on his face. What on Earth could this woman want from me? Maybe she just enjoys showing off her boat as much as small boat owners do. No matter what the reason, my heartbeat was certainly purring along at an elevated rate. As we reached Calypso, I used a ploy to make good a reason to return to Katz Meow.

"Jeez, I've lost my wallet. It's got to be on the yacht. I'll run back over and see if it's there. Be right back."

I knew my wallet was onboard Calypso in my change basket on a shelf above my berth. I figured the truth here might sound too weird to even relate to my crew. Besides, the mystery and excitement of my little escapade was heightened by this late night visit to Katz being clandestine. I walked quickly down the boardwalk and back up the gangplank.

"Welcome back Sir, the Steward announced.

"I'll show you to the main salon."

Nervously, wondering what in the Hell this was all about, I followed him back to the same door where I had briefly spoken with the spectacular woman in white. The Steward opened the door and closed it behind me as I entered. The room was exquisite, with priceless furnishings, original oil paintings, indirect mood lighting, and soft jazz emanating from concealed wall speakers. There was a perfumed smell in the air as if in a high dollar gift boutique and the overall appearance was indicative of the private quarters of an oil sheik or head of state. Trying to find a seat I wouldn't look too out of place on, as if there were any that plebian, I sat down on what appeared to be an overstuffed lazyboy. No one was in the room except me. My host was nowhere to be found. After a few minutes, I began to feel very comfortable. I could get used to this every evening. I'm not sure I even heard the door leading aft from the salon open. I turned my head from staring at a fabulous painting of what must have been two sloops competing in a turn of the century America's Cup duel. I was now looking directly at the full body in front of me. Startled, I nearly fell out of the seat. There, two feet from me was the lady in white, only she was no longer in white. She was wearing a shear black, floor length negligee, covering the scantiest of black satin panties and no bra. She had combed her dark auburn hair back behind her head and the perfume she was wearing was getting me light headed. I was momentarily without speech or thought.

"Well, Captain. I see you have taken me up on my offer to show you around. Or, did you really lose something on board?"

I stammered back.

"No, I mean, yes, I would really love to see more of Katz Meow. Is she yours?"

"She is now. She used to belong to my late husband, Arthur Katz. Perhaps you've heard of him?"

"No, I can't say as I have. I imagine I should have, that is, if I knew much about people who have made a lot of money doing something I don't have a clue about."

"Well, no matter. Arthur was a nice man, a very good provider, but still, quite a bore. I had to force him to buy this little boat to have a diversion from his work. I guess I should feel some responsibility for what happened to him, falling overboard last year. Such a tragedy. You'd have figured that anyone who had lived to be eighty-two years old would have learned to swim at some point. So sad. I miss him, some days."

I didn't know whether she was being straight with me or poking fun at me. Her dialogue sounded like it was out of a forty's detective movie. All we needed here was Bogie to come in wearing a trench coat and light a cigarette for her. She couldn't be a day over forty, still incredibly beautiful and if she was really married to an eighty-year-old man, I could at least see where he was coming from.

"I'm sorry to hear about that. So, you're"

I paused and took a breath.

"a widow, then?"

"Yes, I'm in mourning. As you can see, I still wear black, most nights. Here, Captain, why don't you let me give you a tour? What is your name darling?"

"Les, Les Pendleton. I really appreciate your being willing to show me around this fabulous boat. I've always wondered what they were like on board. From what I've seen so far, they're certainly more than I even expected."

"That's so sweet of you, Les. Here, take my hand and let's start, back this way."

I could barely hold her hand for all of the oversized diamonds and other jewelry that adorned her fingers. I was completely dumbfounded as to what I was doing here and why she wanted to take my hand, but hey, this was supposed to be an adventure and if this is where it was leading, there had to be some higher purpose that it was satisfying. Who was I to question all this? I took her hand as she stopped in front of a highly polished, solid mahogany door with gold knobs and striker plates. She waited for me to open it. As I did so, she stepped forward into another room straight out of a French chateau. It would have fit perfectly in Biltmore. This room however, was a little nerve-racking, for centered against the far wall sat a Louis the Fourteenth canopied bed, made of polished wood and covered with hand carved cherubs and flowers. The canopy was lace and the entire room constituted a master suite the likes of which James Bond never entered. She dropped my hand and walked towards the bed, shedding the floor length negligee as she walked. She was now wearing only the satin black panties and a smile. She looked like the proverbial Playmate of the Year and she was indicating for me to approach her, with a finger curling sexily back towards the bed.

"Les, here, take off some of your clothing and rub my back a little won't you? All of this boat stuff is so grueling. Some nights on board, I ache, terribly. Won't you help me?"

It didn't take a rocket scientist to tell that she was wanting a lot more than a back rub. I froze in my tracks. I kept thinking, "there has to be cameras somewhere in the room. I'm on Candid Camera and I'm going to be a complete idiot. While standing immobile, not knowing just how I should respond, even if I had the common sense and ability to resist such an invitation, she came over to me and started to unbutton my shirt. I wanted to say no, but after all, I am just a man. I'm weak and at times, I'm stupid, I guess. I let her have her way with me. Soon, like Louis the Fourteenth, Fifteenth, Sixteenth and whatever other numbers had succumbed to the weakness of the flesh on this bed, I partook of four hours of the most incredible lovemaking I had ever imagined in my wildest dreams, and I have had some pretty wild dreams."

The sun felt good on my face, it was warming all over simultaneously. No, that wasn't it. It was warm water all over me and bubbling all around me. It was morning; I was in the hot tub on the aft deck of Katz Meow. I quickly scanned the tub water to see if I was alone. Yes, the only sign of the previous evening's sordid affair was the pair of black satin panties floating just beneath the surface of the water. I was planning my escape, wondering where my clothes where and my God, what must they think on Calypso? I left, supposedly to go fetch my wallet and didn't come home at all. By now, the Coast Guard could be dragging Taylor's Creek for my body. I had to get back to the boat. But, where the Hell where my clothes? I really hoped I wouldn't have to go back to Miss Katz's stateroom to find them. It was about that moment that the Steward showed up with a white robe draped over one arm and a Bloody Mary in his other hand.

"Good morning, Sir. Miss Katz will be sleeping in this morning. Your clothes, well, they were a bit soiled, so they are in the ship's laundry and will be ready in about an hour I would imagine. I'll bring them to you."

I knew I couldn't stay here another hour with my crew thinking I was dead.

"Look, I'll come back and get them, or someone could run them over to Calypso on "B" dock. I've got to get back to my boat."

"Certainly, Sir. I'll bring them myself. Feel free to just keep the robe. Miss Katz has them specially made as sort of a ship's souvenir for certain, how shall I say this, special friends. They are quite nice."

"Yes, it truly is. Thanks, I'll be running now."

The main boardwalk was already busy with charter-boat skippers taking tourists fishing, and the early-riser crowd out jogging or walking their golden retrievers. I have to admit, I stood out considerably among the group as I walked down the dock wearing a white terry cloth robe with four inch high letters reading Katz Meow on the breast. I kinda' felt like it should read, "yacht groupie" or better yet "Katz Nip". It was embarrassing to say the least. I was hoping against all odds that John and Essie had gone to bed early and hadn't gotten up yet. Yeah, they wouldn't even know I didn't get in. As I gently stepped aboard, the first greeting came from John Silver, walking up behind me.

"Morning Cappy, I see you've gotten you some high dollar foul weather gear there. Pretty snazzy, I'd say."

"Uh, morning, John. Well, I, er, uh...."

"No need to explain nothin' to me, Cappy. I've shopped at that same store so many times I can't remember. A blue water skipper can't have too much foul weather gear, now can he?"

He knew. Of course, he knew. What other explanation could there possibly be? Only one last obstacle to face. Yep, I could smell the fresh coffee coming out of Calypso's galley. I stepped down the companionway steps, sheepishly. As usual, bright eyed and cheerful as always, Essie stood by the galley counter preparing a gourmet breakfast.

"Morning Cappy, eggs coming right up. I would imagine you might be needing some coffee. Here you go. Put a little Baileys in it already. I knew you'd be out most of the night looking for your wallet."

"You did?"

"Of course, you had overlooked it apparently, sitting right where you usually leave it, in your key basket beside your berth. Found it about two minutes after you left. I like the new jacket. Pretty fancy."

They both knew. OK, they had me. Why did I feel so much like a kid caught with his hand in the candy jar?

"I'll be right back. I want to go slip on some jeans."

"Sure, Cappy, but don't let your eggs get cold."

I could have sworn, as I reached the cockpit heading back to my aft cabin, that she quietly said something to the effect "typical". But, I couldn't be sure she was talking about me, so I didn't bring it back up.

As we went about the task of getting Calypso ready to leave, I couldn't help but look over my shoulder towards Katz and wonder just what happened over there. I could see that they were also getting ready to leave. The white uniformed crew was scrambling about and the lines were being removed from the pilings. Her diesels were running and vibrating down the length of the dock. I tried to not look interested and in fact, did not turn around as I heard the engines rev to leave the port. It was John who brought to my attention that I might want to turn around.

"Cappy, I believe your tailor is leaving."

I turned around and there, leaning against the stern rail was Miss Katz. God, I don't even know her first name. Anyhow, she was looking regal with a white jogging suit, suitably monogrammed with the gold Katz emblem. She had a Bloody Mary in one hand, a silk scarf in the other. The always present Steward was beside her, looking to be at attention. She glanced over to where I was, and while looking directly at me, she pulled the scarf to her mouth and blew me a kiss. She then nonchalantly turned to look at the harbor and in less than a minute, Katz Meow began to grow smaller. About an hour passed. I looked back over towards the long empty finger-pier where the super yacht had been moored and it was almost as if none of the past evening had been real. It was so far off the norm for me that it was more like I was remembering a scene from a movie. Well, I would catalog and store it in my brain to reflect upon on some distant night. Right now, there were things to do.

Chapter Six

There was a strong northerly wind running down the coast. The waves offshore were supposed to be less than five feet, so we came to the decision that we should run offshore to Wrightsville Beach, North Carolina, just above the South Carolina state line. The Intracoastal Waterway offered safe inshore passages but took twice as long to travel as it did going via the ocean. Offshore sailing was more like 'as the crow flies' compared to the winding inland channel. We could make Wrightsville in about eight hours in a strong wind such as this, and to tell the truth, we all wanted to feel the boat in the ocean. That's where real sailors went to test their metal. We double and triple checked everything on deck, topped off the fuel and water tanks, and had one last hot coffee and Baileys. With a brisk northerly breeze, it would be quite chilly out on the ocean.

We dressed warmly and topped it all off with foul weather jackets. The diesel was fired up, the dock lines untied and we pulled away from the city docks. I loved Beaufort, the city made famous in the best-selling novel, Widow-Walk. She had been enticing and entertaining as usual. This may have been the most memorable visit ever. As we pulled out into the middle of Taylor's Creek, we decided to go ahead and raise the mainsail and tuck a reef into her as it would certainly be easier on the calm water here than offshore in five foot seas. If it turned out to be flatter offshore than expected, it would be easy to let out the reef point. With the wind coming from a northerly direction, we would be able to keep the sails full as we headed out to sea. I turned Calypso into the wind, John and Essie raised and reefed the main and we turned back away from the wind and motor-sailed towards the inlet. From the city docks to the actual inlet was less than a mile. Once we left Taylor's Creek, we turned to port and headed into the ever expanding waters of the inlet. Tall breaking waves were pushing up a sheet of white spray on both sides of the inlet. We were immediately running over four foot swells but they weren't breaking in the channel. We all strained to look beyond the inlet to the open water to determine just how rough it was going to be out there. We unfurled the staysail and with Calypso's ten tons of displacement, the diesel running smoothly and sails tight as ticks, she had the power to easily push through the swells. After a half a mile of bow-burying in the inlet swells, which were fairly close together, the ocean appeared to be a little rough but nothing to worry about. There was a sprinkling of breaking waves giving a white top to about every fourth or fifth wave and blowing some chilly spray across our decks. Inside the cockpit enclosure, and with our heavy clothing on, we were quite dry and comfortable. The movement of a sailboat in the ocean as she rises and falls graciously over the swells is a completely different dance than the motion in the sounds and rivers inshore. The inshore waves are generally close together due to the shallowness of the water. This causes a continual bucking action of the hull that can be very uncomfortable and wet. The large ocean swells, over much deeper water are further apart and cause the boat to rise and fall much more smoothly. The deeper the water, the better the motion. Any blue water sailor will tell you that in severe weather, you should head to deep water. Today, we would head out about four miles to get away from the shore effect, which causes the waves to get closer and steeper. We were sideways to the waves as we headed out, which caused Calypso to roll considerably. It was therefore a big relief when we were sufficiently offshore enough to turn south and head towards our destination. This put the waves directly to our stern. It still caused some roll, but not nearly so severe. The wind was off our starboard quarter and this allowed us to keep both sails out to the port side and not have to run wing and wing, with the headsail out to one side and the main to the other. That requires a lot more attention to the wheel. On Calypso it wouldn't allow the use of the autopilot which just isn't sensitive enough to handle the constant steering adjustments needed to keep both sails full. There's also the possibility of an accidental jibe, probably the most dangerous unplanned sailing event. This is caused when the wind is behind the boat and changes slightly from one side of the hull to the other. The mainsail, complete with its massive aluminum boom will fly across the deck of the boat at warp speed to stay with the changing wind direction. Many deaths and gear failures have occurred as a direct result of this scenario. For those reasons, it has always been my least favorite point of sail. With the present wind direction we didn't have that concern. Calypso was steaming along, a bone in her teeth, making seven knots as she walked up and over the large swells. We were all beaming aboard. This is the moment we had been waiting for. We were at sea, headed south and all was well with us and the world. With everything stable and the ride comfortable, we began to relax and get to know each other a little better.

"Essie," I began,

"So, what is your story?"

"What do you want to know?"

"Well, you're pretty much a mystery woman to me right now. I know you're a great cook, a good sailor and a terrific dancer. But where do you come from? Been married? How many times? Any kids? Criminal record? Outstanding warrants? You know, the usual."

"Pretty darned nosy, aren't you?"

"Absolutely! Now, spill it."

"Well, I'm from Texas by way of Michigan and Wisconsin. Got pregnant at seventeen and tried to make a go of it. My choice of men, if you call a seventeen year old's hormone map a choice, turned out to be the road to disaster. Within five years, I had a daughter, a son, and an alcoholic husband. We had moved to North Carolina where he had family to mooch off and help him get out of jail or whatever trouble he was in at the moment. It was tough going for a long time. I was the only one that could be counted on to make a living, pay the bills, help the kids, whatever. I finally had enough, divorced him and raised the kids on my own. They're grown now and I'm starting over, a lot wiser I might mention at this point. I'm reasonably happy and determined to enjoy my life from here on out. I know one thing for certain, I can spot a loser from a mile away."

"And how did you wind up a sailor?"

"In Racine, Wisconsin, there was a lighthouse just down the street from our house. It was overlooking Lake Michigan. It was the Wind Point lighthouse. I could look out my bedroom window and see it, night and day. It looked so beautiful and seemed to be beckoning me to head out to sea. It was very romantic to watch. When we moved to Carolina, my in-laws had a sailboat that we went out on occasionally. They kept it in New Bern. I loved the time on that boat and New Bern. When the last child moved out, I knew that's where I would go, at least for starters."

"And no man in your life at the moment?"

"Nope, not looking either."

"Well, what about the Joe Namath thing the other night?"

"A short term experiment. And a complete failure. I'm not really looking for any permanent man in my life, so it makes me a little too independent to get along with for most guys. Men all want 'the little woman' and that I'm not. I've taken care of myself and my kids, bought a house, made a good living. I don't need anybody to help me do crap. I'm perhaps a little jaded about men right now. I'm just looking to have a little fun and adventure. Isn't that what you said you wanted? So, we're not that different, are we? Why, I even have a bathrobe like yours. It doesn't have the gold monogram on it, but other than that, it's the same."

"Touché! I deserved that. Remind me to tell you about that some time."

"I'd personally rather not hear about it."

I was a little shocked that Essie seemed to be somehow offended by my indiscretion the previous evening. I guess it just made me look like another shiftless man, looking for a pair of silk panties to get into. I turned to John.

"OK, Long John, fill us in on your sordid past. I KNOW you've got some interesting skeletons left in many a closet."

"There ain't a whole lot about me that most folks would find interesting. I guess the thing I'm most proud of is I ain't never held any job longer than a year. Every time I start to feel like I'm settling down, my feet start to get real itchy and I just have to move along. I've never had any money much, but I ain't never been hungry, without a roof over my head, if I wanted one. I've been just about everywhere I ever wanted to go and done everything I ever wanted to do and truth be told, some things I shouldn't a done. I'd have to say, of everything I've done and the places I've been, I've never been more content and happy than I am when I'm doing just what we're doing right now. For me, the open sea, a good boat, a fair wind and a good crew are the best things in life."

"You ever been married?"

"All I'll say to that question is yes. Next question."

"Sore subject with you too?"

"Like I said, next question."

"You said you were in prison for a while. What prison where you in?"

"Sing Sing."

"I wouldn't think they would put some one there just for being behind in their alimony payments."

"They don't. That time, I was just in the county lockup over in Burgaw, North Carolina."

"That time? How many times have you been in prison?"

"Enough to know I ain't going back. Look, you don't need to worry about me. I ain't never hurt anybody and the worst crime I ever did was just being around the wrong folks at the wrong time. Truth be told, I was passed out drunk in the back seat of a car when the two guys I had been running around with decided to rob a liquor store. They wrecked the car when the cops started chasing us and I woke up with handcuffs on. Did three years for that little drunk. I found out, drink with sailboaters and the worst thing that can happen to you is you wake up on somebody else's boat. Can you identify with that, Cappy?"

"You're damn right, John."

"How bad was it, being in Sing Sing?"

"I normally don't like to talk about it, but since you asked, it's not someplace I'll ever go again. I think it helped me in a lot of ways. It made me appreciate the fact that all the good things there are, are just sitting out here waiting for you. You don't need a bunch of money or power to share in all the best of this world. We got it right out here, right now. This is what it's all about, Cappy. I'll never let myself be put in a situation to not be able to be where I want, when I want. That's the worst thing about prison. Hell, I finished my college education in prison, thanks to Uncle Sam."

"You graduated from college?"

"Sure did. You're looking at a full fledged history graduate. Love to read about the Revolutionary War. That was my favorite. I know all of Washington's staff and all the major battles by heart. Still like to read about it."

"Damn, John. You're just one surprise after another."

"If you knew everything about everybody you know something about, you'd surely be scared to be around most of 'em. Sing Sing had a lot of guys with an education in there. You could find an expert on just about everything if you took the time to get to know them. I still call some of my old mates up from time to time when I have a problem. Gotten' some good advice, I have."

"I'm impressed. Well, had you noticed that the wind seems to be picking up a little?"

"Sure have. Could be in for quite a blow. How far along are we?"

I punched in the waypoint for Wrightsville Inlet in the GPS and determined the distance to be about eighteen miles.

We're a little over half way there. You think the single reef in the main is enough?"

Essie looked over the sails and immediately responded.

"Nope, the rule is, when you first ask yourself if you need another reef, you need another one, right then. You head her up, Cappy. John and I will handle it."

I turned Calypso into the wind and waves. It then became apparent just how right Essie was. The wind was up to around twenty-five knots steady and the seas looked to be running between six and eight feet. That meant that when you were in the bottom of a trough between waves, they appeared to be twelve to sixteen feet above your head. Thank God, they were still quite a distance apart. That would allow Calypso, with her speed properly adjusted, to run up and over their backs without slamming into the next one. In just a few moments, they had the sail trimmed and I turned Calypso back away from the wind. Since we were running with the wind at around seven knots, about eight and half miles per hour, it reduced the apparent wind, which is the wind you can actually feel on your face, to around eighteen knots. That is still a very fresh breeze. Though I knew Calypso well, John and Essie were just beginning to develop their impressions of her.

"She's a very stiff boat, Cappy. I believe she'll stand upright with this double in the main till the wind gets up to about thirty five knots."

Essie seemed to know more about sail trim than either of us.

"When it hits thirty, you need to go to a triple reefed main and the storm staysail. You don't want to loose balance on the wheel by continually just shortening the main."

She was right on target. I first noticed the black squall line bearing down on us only a minute later. There were lighting flashes within it and the coloring went from dark gray to dark green. History has shown me that a dark green cloud means a very intense storm. The tops of the clouds were chopped off indicating extremely high winds. This was going to be a serious blow.

"Essie, this time you take the wheel and John, you help me secure the main completely and we'll just continue under the storm staysail alone."

"Aye, Cappy. Let's do it now for it gets any worse."

We both moved forward, after securing our harnesses to the tether post just forward of the cockpit. The deck was already moving up and down at a pretty severe angle. I'd guess the wave heights at about ten feet by this time. Still, they weren't breaking yet and the motion was predictable. We lowered the main entirely and lashed it to the boom with the bitter end of the jiffy reef line. By the time this was accomplished and we were back in the cockpit, the wind was hitting forty knots on the wind-speed indicator. Essie surrendered the wheel to me and said,

"Cappy, I'll go below and make sure everything is secure. Don't want any hatches left unlocked or anything that could fall over and get broken below."

"Sounds good, Essie. Brace yourself, don't bang your head on anything down there."

"Don't worry about me, Cappy. I've got my sealegs."

John looked over at me.

"This is gonna' be a strong one, Cappy. Just as well we

test ourselves right here as anywhere. Ain't the first one of these I've seen and it sure as Hell ain't gonna' be the last, I hope."

The sky turned into night though it was only four PM. The waves running up behind us appeared to be as high as the foothills in the Blue Ridge mountains I had been to so many times. They would move right over our stern and look like they were going to spill over us, or poop us as the old salts would call it. At the last second, Calypso would rise like a roller coaster on its way back up from a steep drop. The stern would jump up to the top of the wave and it would run harmlessly under us. Occasionally, just before we hit the top, we would slide back down the backside of the wave like a surfer would if he missed a wave. But, when we actually caught the wave, our speed on those dives had to be fifteen knots or better. We'd run down the wave a short distance till we found a less steep section and then it would run under us also. It's what the old New Englanders called a Nantucket Sleigh Ride. Calypso handled this as if she had been specifically bred for it. I was growing fonder of her with each wave she mastered. I have to say, none of us seemed to actually be scared. We knew what we had to do and realized that thousands of boats before us had been exactly where we were now and that if we managed the boat properly, we would be fine. And we were.

Within twenty minutes, the worst of the squall had passed. I took a GPS reading to determine what the storm had done to our progress. I was absolutely delighted to discover that we had made almost eight miles to the good since our last check. We were only ten miles from Wrightsville Beach. However, we were just a few days out of New Bern on our journey and conventional cruising wisdom was proving to be correct. October was too early in the fall to be heading south. Hurricane season wouldn't be officially over till November and nor'easters were continually running south along with us. If we kept pressing our luck, we would eventually get hit with a really bad one. We needed to be very careful in picking our battles with Mother Nature. She could win anytime she wanted to and tweaking her nose wasn't advisable.

We experienced another smaller and less powerful squall with this front. We weren't nearly as anxious as this one approached. The first in a series of squalls is generally the worst. By six P.M. we were anchored safely inside of the inlet at Wrightsville Beach. As soon as you clear the inlet, a sharp turn to starboard will put you into a marvelous anchorage called Banks Channel. It's deep, protected, and offers a panoramic view of highly developed Wrightsville Beach. After a bite of dinner and a nightcap, we all turned into our berths. I was nestled snuggly in my aft cabin, reading a copy of Cruising World and listening to the harmonica music coming from Essie's berth in the next cabin. She was a pretty amazing woman.

Sunrise came quickly, and brought with it some more surprising developments. I don't know why I thought the cruising life would be simple. No sooner had I cut on the VHF radio to check the weather, than I received a hail from Seapath Marina, only about a half mile or so from where we anchored. In a nutshell, they informed me that I had a visitor waiting for me at their docks. When I asked to put him on, they related that he was not there at the moment but indicated that he would be there by the time we arrived. Somewhat hesitant, I agreed to motor over after we had eaten breakfast. My first thought, a land thought, was that it had to be a lawyer there to serve divorce papers on me for my wife. Though I generally disdain any business contacts with attorneys (my experiences had always been bad) I figured that I didn't want to spend any time worrying about what might be. I'd face the music right while the piper was playing the tune. I can't stand the dread of not knowing what bad thing may or may not be waiting for me. Let's get it over with.

True to my word, we were shortly tying up at Seapath, a very high dollar condominium project where you had to buy your boat slip as well as your condo. The average slip cost more than my boat. I had wondered around the place a few times in the past to look at boats. I knew it was all way beyond my means. The dockmaster came out to greet me with a note in hand. Before I could even read it, another visitor arrived, wearing what appeared to be a limo driver's uniform. He stood by while I read.

"Captain Les, I will be joining you aboard Calypso for dinner. You did invite me, did you not? In so much as, you know how I like things extremely Bristol aboard, I have arranged for a detailing crew to spiff up your yacht while you and your crew take a limo tour of beautiful Wilmington, lunch included. Please don't disappoint me.

Melinda Katz"

Essie and John, quizzical, as one might imagine, came over to ask what the heck was going on. Essie asked first.

"And this is supposed to be what?"

"You don't want to know."

"I'd be willing to bet you I already know. It's not like all of your friends are sending chauffeur driven limos to meet us in every port, now is it? I'm certain I hear a purrrr in here somewhere, don't I?"

I have to admit I was more than pleased to detect in Essie, the slightest tinge of being upset about this development. There was a certain degree of electricity developing between Essie and I though neither of us had addressed it in any way. As we were deciding what to do, a large white van appeared next to the limo with the words Mr. Marine Clean on the side. Two guys and two women jumped out and strode past us towards Calypso. The straggliest of the group said.

"Yup, that's her. Bill, you and I can take the topsides. Jennie, you and Bev do the interior. We got two hours, let's move!"

Essie could see what was going on here.

"You know, we take this ride and tonight you'll be the one furnishing 'a ride' if you get my drift."

"Essie, are you trying to say that I would be giving up my right to choose, if I accepted any form of appreciation from Melinda?"

"Oh, it's Melinda now, is it?"

"I would consider her a friend, wouldn't you? When was the last time someone who wasn't your friend sent a limo to take you to lunch while they cleaned up your place?"

"That's just my point. In the real world, it never happens to anyone, period."

"I say, we just let this nice man drive us downtown where we can have a great lunch, look at Wilmington and then we come back to a quiet dinner on board a Bristol boat. You can meet Miss Katz and be in a better position to make any judgments about her. What do you say to that?"

"Hey, it's your boat and your life, pal. I'm just the crew."

Once again, I was relishing in the apparent sense of competition that Essie was showing here. Perhaps, she was a little attracted to me. I certainly had more than a passing attraction to her. I mean, a woman who loves sailboats? Come'on."

The driver motioned for us, and the disheveled crew of the soon to be clean Calypso headed downtown.

Wilmington, for those of you that might not be aware, is one of the premier cities in the country for filming motion pictures. There is a major studio there and over a hundred feature films have been made there. A few worthy of mentioning are, BLUE VELVET, the David Lynch masterpiece, YEAR OF THE DRAGON, the NINGA TURTLE films, WEEKEND AT BERNIES, a personal favorite of mine, NO MERCY and many others. It has a big city feel to the place while maintaining its old Southern charm. I like the town. The driver pulled up to the front door of one of the city's best-known watering holes down on Front Street. I had always wanted to eat there, but it was not within the parameters of my frivolity budget so it had never occurred. I leaned over to the driver and casually whispered,

"is, uh, er, uh…Miss Katz..er, uh.."

To which, he courteously responded without hesitation,

"let me interrupt you for just a moment, Captain. Before it slips my mind, Miss Katz said that your entire afternoon was 'on her' so, I will be picking up your check as you leave and will be standing by right here. Now, you were saying, Captain?"

"Oh, I was just wondering if the service here was pretty quick. Wouldn't want to be late getting back to the boat to pay the cleaning crew."

"Miss Katz has already paid the cleaning crew, Captain.

So, take as long as you want."

This guy was good, I mean, really good. He could sense a situation and come up with the right solution with very little input from the participants. I felt bad just walking away and leaving him sitting in the car while we went in to eat.

"Driver."

"Yes, Captain?"

"What is your name?"

"Carlos, Carlos Vernandis. My friends call me Carlo."

"Carlo, we want you to come inside and eat with us. How about it?"

"Well, I couldn't, Captain."

He was dumbfounded. It was obvious this scenario didn't occur very often.

"Yes, you can. As a matter of fact, I insist that you join us."

"Well, Captain, if you insist. Miss Katz did say to do whatever you wanted."

"It's settled then."

"Yes, Sir. I'll park the car around the corner and be right in."

"That's great, we'll get a table."

By the time Carlo entered, we were seated in what could only be described as a 'priority' table, near the fireplace and with a spectacular view of the entire restaurant. It was much like what you would expect on Sunset Boulevard in Los Angeles. The restaurant's front consisted entirely of large french windows so that the underprivileged could peer in and be extremely envious which, after all is the entire point of being rich and famous, am I right? There were a few, artsy fartsy paintings on the wall that a six-year-old with a ruler, food coloring and a water-pistol could create in a half hour. The prices on them indicated that these must have been painted by Picasso's kids. There were a lot of folks coming and going, some dressed to the nines and others who looked as bad as we did. I think its kind of neat how the grubby look is in. For the first time in my life, I'm stylish. Old blue jeans with an unintentional rip in the knee, paint stains from working on the boat, an old blue denim work shirt with matching paint stains, a boat cap, a foul weather jacket and voila', there you have the ultimate yachting fashion statement of our time. Of course, having your uniformed, limo driver at your table lent a certain elite air to our group, even though it may have been confusing to others as to why he was at the table with us. I tried to look benevolent, yet stately. It was working. I felt one with the joint until the inevitable happened and I blew it.

He just came in the front door, all by himself and was seated at the small table on the other side of the fire, right beside us. I couldn't believe it. Mr. Easy Rider himself, Dennis friggin' Hopper! I tried to be nonchalant and casually leaned over to the middle of the table and motioned for everyone to meet me there. With a circle of four heads meeting in the middle, I'm sure it looked as if we were calling a play of some sort. I whispered.

"Do you see who just sat down beside us?"

Essie glanced over,

"Yeah, it's Dennis Hopper. Looks older than I remembered him."

I couldn't contain my fawning much longer.

"Did you see him in SPEED? Man, he does the psychos so friggin' great. I just love that guy. I wonder is he filming a movie here. Think it would be all right to just walk over and say 'hi, Dennis, I'm a fan?'"

Once again, Carlo came to the rescue.

"Sir, if you don't mind, I handle this sort of thing all the time for Miss Katz, though it's usually a somewhat reversed situation. Would you like for me to arrange for you to meet Mr. Hopper?"

"Would I? That would be unbelievable. Carlo, I owe you, man."

Carlo got up, placed his uniform cap under his arm and in the most professional manner you could possibly imagine, wondered over to the table containing my hero. Dennis Hopper smiled pleasantly as Carlo approached. Carlo bent forward and whispered something in Hopper's ear. He then stood by as the Hollywood icon stood up, grabbed his wineglass, put his arm around Carlo and walked over to our table. He looked me directly in the eye.

"Captain, Les. Mind if I join you and your crew for lunch? Melinda told me all about you at her party the other night aboard that cruise liner she calls her boat. I'd been looking forward to meeting you. From what she says, you're quite the sailor."

He KNEW my name. DENNIS HOPPER KNEW MY FRIGGIN' NAME. Everybody in the entire place was watching as he put his arm around my shoulder, gave me a little star-like hug and sat down between me and Essie.

"And this beautiful young woman is?"

God, I was trying not to stammer. I felt like a contestant on The Price Is Right who couldn't remember whether vacuum cleaners sold for fifty bucks or two thousand. Stay calm, this is one of those once in a lifetime moments.

"Essie, I'm Essie, Dennis. May I call you Dennis?"

"I'd be disappointed if you didn't. And you are?"

He looked over at John Silver.

"John, John Silver, Mr. Hopper, I mean, Dennis, sir."

He studied John for a moment.

"I could swear we've met before. Ever spend any time in the Venice Beach area of Los Angeles?"

"Well, I've been to California before, might say I did a little time there, but no, not at Venice Beach. Sounds interesting though. Hey, man. I loved EASY RIDER. I'm sure you've heard that a million times, but I just feel like if I don't tell you, I'll wish I did later, back on the boat."

My curiosity was killing me.

"What are you doing here Dennis, making a movie?"

"I have a home here. Actually an apartment, right down this street a little ways. I love Wilmington. Came here to film BLUE VELVET and bought a place. It was kind of like the place that was responsible for the rebirth of my film career. I was coming back after my, well, let's just call it my days of youthful indiscretions. My old friend Fred Caruso was producing BLUE VELVET and asked me to be the bad guy, surprise, huh? I fell for the whole area. Come here all the time. You sure we haven't met before, John? You look just like somebody I've seen before. Never mind, it will come to me later."

Two hours later, after much laughter, lie swapping and wine sampling which turned to beer guzzling, it was time to go. This had been an unbelievable experience. I never thought I'd ever meet someone like him, and especially never thought I'd share a meal with him, buddy-like, you know. We all walked out together. Dennis, yeah, I call him that now, walked out with me, arm around my shoulder, gave Essie a big hug and a kiss which was pretty darned aggressive, well, never mind, he's an actor. Then, one last time, he put an arm around John Silver and said,

"It'll come to me, you'll see. Well guys, this has been great fun for me. If you visit with Melinda much while she's in the area, I'm sure our paths will cross again."

Carlo drove up in the limo and we all hopped aboard for the trip back to Seapath and Calypso. I was actually overcome with the uniqueness of the day.

"You know, this trip was meant to be. There's just too much going on here. I can't put my finger on any one thing, but all this, it's almost has a mystical quality to it. And today, lunch with a friggin' Hollywood legend? That's just a little too much to believe."

Essie offered up.

"Dennis, was nice. I liked him. Seems like just about everybody knows your friend, Miss Katz, doesn't it?"

We drove back through the heart of old Wilmington. Market Street was completely covered with mammoth hundred year old oak trees that shaded the entire street. On either side were magnificent colonial mansions dating back to the glory days of the old south. Scarlet Ohara would have fit right in on these sidewalks. I personally, never wanted to own another house or even a piece of property to take care of in my entire life. If I never mowed another blade of grass or painted a porch again, it would be too soon. All of that 'own your own home' crap is just a bunch of hooey. It just turns you into a slave of the bank, the power company, the insurance company, the water department, city and county taxes and the count continues. You never own one of the son of bitches. If you had it paid for completely and didn't pay your real estate taxes to the REAL owner, you'd see how fast you'd be on the street. Well, I didn't own one anymore. My ex did and she could burn it for all I cared. I was at home and at peace on Calypso. This cruise was shaping up to be more than just a way to escape a hostile world. It was beginning to become an adventure. I loved it. A little nervous, but loving it just the same. It all seemed too surreal. I mean, I walked out of my life about a week ago, met a lot of great folks, had some fabulous sailing, made it through two pretty good storms, met a damned beautiful woman, who for some reason was attracted to me and then, topped it all off doing lunch with Dennis Hopper. And yet, I was still only a two-hour drive from the world I was leaving behind. So far, I had no regrets.

Carlo pulled us over to the Seapath gate. We all thanked him profusely. He refused my offer of a five-dollar bill. Sure, I'm embarrassed to have offered so little, but you have to remember it represented almost two percent of everything I owned. I think two percent is right. Anyhow, we walked down the slip and found Calypso, shining like a new penny. She had never looked that good in all the years I had owned her. I kept her straight, mechanically and structurally sound, and well, presentable is probably the best word to use here. Given the choice, sail, drink beer with friends, listen to Jimmy Buffett and make pina-colladas or clean the boat, you know the answer. But now, Jeez, she looked like new. The inside was even more impressive. They had polished the brass clock, barometer and gimbaled cabin lights to the point they looked like store display models. It would have been difficult to find a nook or cranny that had not been detailed. It was difficult to understand why so many things seemed to be going right. That is not a pattern that my life history had grown to expect. It was beginning to make me feel like it was time for the other shoe to fall. Essie, now that we were onboard, by the way, did I mention how sexy she looked today? Well, she did. Anyway, now that we were onboard, she took over the ship's duties for the evening.

"Well, since the benefactor of our appearance today on Hollywood Squares, is coming to dinner, I guess I better try and figure out something to cook. Now, what really special can I make with two pounds of hamburger meat and a box of red beans and rice? Hmmmhhh...let me think. Oh yes, we still have a case and a half of Coronas. That's comforting."

Thinking was not going to be needed, after-all. In the midst of Essie's irritability, appeared Carlo.

"Captain Les, I have a note here from Miss Katz."

He stood by as I read it to the crew.

"Dear Captain Les and the crew of Calypso. I regret that I will be unable to attend our planned soiree this evening. Pressing matters have appeared that will cause me to head south a little sooner than planned. I am most certain we will reach another port together in the near future. All my best.

M. Katz"

I have to admit there was disappointment in my voice as I

told everyone,

"Well, we can get a good night's rest tonight. We're on an absolutely pristine ship, thanks to Melinda and we all had a wonderful day. Now Essie, did you say something about us having meat loaf and red beans with rice? Ummmmhhhh! I'll be glad to help, where's that Corona?"

I opened a cold beer and set down on the settee across from the galley and just watched Essie throw together the meal. She was a very energetic young woman. I don't know why I thought she might have any interest in me. First, I wasn't even divorced, or legally separated for that matter. Second, I was almost fifty and she was about thirty-eight, an attractive thirty-eight. She was the kind of woman who didn't have to do anything to be attractive, at least to me. No make-up, hair just quickly brushed back, her very fit, trim body tucked into tight jeans and a sweatshirt, yeah, this was one fine chunk of woman. She was fiery; yet, she was unable to hide a certain sweetness and the feeling that this was a woman who only wants to be treated fairly by her man. Nothing extra, just fairly would be fine. I don't know why any woman would settle for less than that. I have always been a little embarrassed by many of the representatives of my gender. We're not much to look at. As a matter of fact, if we don't keep a razor close by, within a day or two, we look more like animals than people. Two hours worth of any kind of work produces a fairly unattractive, unpleasant smelling creature who thinks it's pretty much appropriate behavior to belch or fart as needed, and that being considerate to their woman was an unparalleled act of human kindness. As long as she didn't want him to do anything for her between the start of Gameday Countdown on Friday night and the end of the Monday Night Football game. Why a woman would find us appealing in any fashion has always been a mystery to me. I just sat there, sipping my beer and watching her cheerfully fix us a meal. John Silver came in and sat down beside me.

"Smells mighty good in here, don't it, Cappy? What day of the week is it? You know, they might have a game on in the marina clubhouse. We could just grab a plate of this fine food and all run up there and see."

I rest my case.

"John, I don't want to have to pay a slip rental here for staying overnight. We need to finish up eating and then head back out to the anchorage. I'd like to start heading south again early in the morning. As beautiful as Wilmington is, I used to keep a boat here and all this doesn't really feel like we've actually left home yet. I'm ready to see some new places. Essie, you sit down here and eat. John and I will clean up the galley. Then, we can motor back out to Banks Channel for the night."

Essie smiled as she did exactly as I had suggested.

"Thanks, guys. I'm not used to getting spoiled like this."

John Silver was still remorseful about the possibility of any missed games.

"You know, I wonder why nobody ever thought of running a twenty four hour a day sports channel over the VHF radio for all of the sailors out here without cable?"

We motored out to the Banks Channel after dinner. We mostly just puttered along, enjoying the view of all Wrightsville Beach's lights playing off the dead calm waters of the channel. On one side of the channel is the outer banks section of the beach and on the other is the mainland. Both sides are highly developed and the light display is magnificent. With all of the reflections on the water for three hundred and sixty degrees, it was a lot like being in the center of the Milky Way. We were a small star in a big galaxy, self sufficient in our own right, but yet a part of something much, much larger.

Chapter Seven

Sunrise appeared through a morning fog around six forty five. It seemed that no matter how early I awoke, Essie and John were always up ahead of me. Coffee would already be brewing and John Silver would be on deck straightening things up for the day's journey. It was a little disconcerting, considering the fact that I could only be described as a morning person. All of our personalities seem to mesh with very few points of contention. There wasn't an 'arguer' among us. We all wanted the same thing, peace, harmony, a stout boat, a good wind, and the freedom to take advantage of them all. Today, after a fairly long motor down the ICW, we would eventually come to the mouth of the Cape Fear River. The Cape Fear is a wide, dark, fast-moving body of water that journeyed from over a hundred miles inland to where it was joining the Atlantic Ocean, just South of some of the worst shoals on the eastern seaboard. The river is one of two all-weather ports on the North Carolina Coast, the other one being Beaufort where we had exited from a few days earlier. We would head offshore here and travel southward in the ocean, re-entering the ICW at Charleston, South Carolina. There, we would check the weather again before deciding whether or not to remain off-shore.

The trip down the ICW was slow and beginning to be a little boring. After a few days of ICW travel, the ocean starts to look like an escape from this 'inland sailor's' highway to Florida. Real sailors wanted to be offshore. The 'ditch' is for wussies. When we reached the intersection of the ICW with the Cape Fear, we left the ditch and headed down-river towards the inlet. The outgoing current was literally screaming out to sea and we motored along at over nine knots speed over the bottom. That represented six knots of boat speed plus three knots of river speed. A last minute check of the weather channel indicated that the predicted nor'easter had not made its way south as of yet and there was more than likely two days of clear weather, even though there would be a twenty to twenty five knot northerly breeze. We would be on a strong broad reach south. We should make Charleston in under forty eight hours. This would be about one half the time required to take the inland route. Of course, it also meant sailing forty-eight hours straight, with crewmembers each taking a watch through the night. By now, I had great confidence in the sea-keeping abilities of my crew. It appeared that I was the least experienced of the three of us.

"So, last chance, John, Essie. Do we jump offshore here or put in at Baldhead Island for the night and pick back up the ICW tomorrow and stay inshore?"

They answered in harmony.

"Offshore, Cappy. Let's head south!"

It was now about two PM and that meant we should arrive off Charleston in the late afternoon on Tuesday. That would give us a daylight approach to their inlet, which I had never seen before. I had, however read all the accounts of the tragic sinking of the Morning Dew in the middle of the night on the rock jetty at the inlet's approach. The Captain and his sons were all killed in the winter grounding. I knew I didn't want to make the entrance after dark. I would stay offshore till sunrise before I'd attempt that. We seemed to have all the elements in our favor. We turned Calypso briefly into the wind before leaving the calm waters of the river and raised the mainsail, setting her up with the number two reef point. With a predicted twenty knots of wind, a double reefed main and the small staysail would be all the power we could want. John quickly made good the mainsail, and almost as an afterthought suggested,

"Cappy, I know it's a little late to think about this, but give me five more minutes. I want to take the inflatable dink off the davits, let the air out and stow it below. I just had a flashback and it's a lot rougher out here."

It was an on target idea. I held her into the wind and in short order there were two empty dinghy davits over the stern. I should have known to do that. No seasoned offshore sailor would ever go into the ocean with a damn dinghy hanging off the back, just begging to either be broken loose and lost or worse yet, swept across the entire deck like a cannonball looking for a target which would most likely be the cockpit enclosure.

Once John had it stowed below, we came about and headed out through the channel. As we broke into open water at the first offshore buoys, we saw a very large container ship in-bound. We stayed as far to the starboard side of the channel as we felt safe and were all a little startled at how fast she closed the distance between us. She had to be moving a minimum of twenty-five knots. That's respectable for most small speedboats. Hard to imagine something over nine hundred feet long moving that fast. We were even more impressed with the wake she put up that was coming straight at us like a tidal wave! It was a good six feet tall. We turned the bow into it at the last second and it still felt like we had struck an iceberg as we pounded into it. A smaller boat, say under thirty-foot could have a serious problem with a wake like that.

It became apparent, very quickly that there were some big

rollers offshore. They were widely spaced and didn't appear to be breaking, but at an average height of five to six feet, as they ran under the boat from the port quarter, the motion was pretty damned sickening. After thirty minutes of this, I had contributed my breakfast to any seagulls that trailed behind us. That helped a little as I tried to ignore the rolling in my stomach that matched the ocean. I looked over at my crew just in time to see Essie handing John Silver another greasy sausage dog! That sight helped me discover another small treasure trove of undigested ham and cheese sandwich. Totally empty felt good. If this rolling motion continued, I simply would not eat till we got to Charleston. I needed to loose a few pounds anyway. To describe the condition called seasick to someone who has never experienced it, try imagining combining the flu with dysentery, add to this an inner ear infection that has you completely dizzy and oh yes, don't forget the gunshot to the belly. That's a fair description I think. Remember those scenes in the movies where the really horrible bad guy tells the good person he has just kidnapped, something to the effect,

"when I'm through with you, you'll be praying for death!"?

That is also a very good description of how you feel after an hour or two of being really seasick. I had been this way a few times before and knew that once I had emptied my gut, if I steered the boat, it would help me get back my equilibrium. So, I relieved Long John who was chomping down his third sausage and egg sandwich while he worked the wheel with his feet.

"What a ride, eh, Cappy? You all right? I gotta' tell you, you don't look so good. You need to head back in? We could turn around, take the ditch south in the morning."

There was no way I could start out like this. If I was going to sea, I had to be able to deal with it.

"Nope, John, I'll be OK, just let me take the wheel."

"Sure, Cappy. If I can get you anything, just holler."

"John."

"Yeah, Cappy?"

"Just go below to finish that sandwich, please!"

Looking somewhat startled that the act of eating his sandwich could possibly be upsetting me, he complied.

"Sure, Cappy. Right away. I'm mostly done anyway."

He turned his back to me for just a second and when he turned back around, he had stuffed the entire remainder, probably three bites into his mouth at once. With both hands raised to show me how empty they now were, and a garbled voice much like a kid who has jammed the entire pack of cookies into his mouth at once, he said,

"theee, all gome!"

Essie came up behind me and asked,

"Does this help or bother you?"

She took her hands and gently worked them on either side of my neck and along the tops of my shoulders. I had to admit, it felt great. It would have felt great whether or not I was sick. Make a note; feigning sickness might get Essie to rub my shoulders.

"Definitely helps."

She continued for about five minutes.

"There, I'll go below and make sure everything is secure before it gets dark."

"Thanks, Essie, that was really nice. I appreciated it, really."

"Sure, Cappy, anytime."

Within an hour or so, I was feeling much better. Now, there was a definite emptiness building in my stomach, but I was flat out afraid to put anything else in it till the ocean quit rolling quite so badly. I would just tough it out. That was going to be a lot 'tougher' than I originally thought. I worked the wheel till about nine PM. That was a good six-hour shift, constantly turning the wheel to offset the rolling waves that kept pushing the boat to starboard. We were now about fifteen miles offshore and thirty miles south of the Cape Fear. We were definitely committed to Charleston as the next possible port. With a very strong northerly wind and the seas running powerfully along with it, we couldn't begin to fight our way back. The good news was, we were making fantastic time. The GPS showed a speed over the bottom of over eight knots on average. That was actually above our normal hull speed, so to say the least, we were booking. I was wearing down. Essie and John both knew what was going on and that soon I would be hitting the wall. John came over to me.

"Feeling better, Cappy?"

"Yeah, as long as I steer and don't eat, I'm fine. Damn, how much longer do you think these swells will last?"

"Well, I'd say long after we get to Charleston. We need this wind to hold just like this to help us get there ahead of that nor'easter they've been talking about. I just listened to the weather station and they're saying it will be off North Carolina late tomorrow evening. We might not be able to totally beat it to Charleston. We need to hold all the speed we can get. There's no where else to put in till we get there. Least no where's that I feel comfortable about trying in this weather. We need an all weather inlet and that's Charleston. Hell, that ain't going to be easy in a nor'easter. So, what I'm saying here is this, you need to try and nibble on some of these ginger snaps I've brought you and keep putting some water down you along with 'em. Dehydration can happen pretty easy when you're barfing so much. Ginger will stop the queasiness and after some rest, I think you could put some food in you. Essie will help you into the cabin. Just lay down and try to sleep. You're definitely going to need some rest by morning."

Essie took me by the arm and led my totally exhausted frame to the bunk in the aft cabin.

"Here, Les, it's pretty chilly, even down here, so you need to keep this comforter pulled up. I'll check on you real often. Try to just get some sleep."

I didn't have to try long. I was out like a light in fifteen seconds. Steering till I was exhausted had seen to that. I was aware throughout the night that Essie had come in and put her hand on my forehead several times, to see if I had a temperature, a sign that I was suffering from more than being seasick. That's all it was. The main problem that develops with someone suffering from severe motion sickness is dehydration from not being able to keep any fluids down, and pure mental exhaustion. I could tell about dawn that I was much stronger. I needed something in me though. Just as I sat up, Essie appeared.

"Cappy, here, let me help you put on some warm clothes. You don't want to try to do anything down here. It'll upset you again. Get these on and let's go topsides. I'll bring you something to eat that's easy on your stomach, cause you need to spell John some and then me. We've been up all night and it's gotten worse out here, a lot worse."

That didn't sound good. At least I felt like I had some of my strength back. I threw on my foul weather jacket and went to the cockpit. The first thing I saw as I approached the light coming through the companionway above was, my God, a wave, maybe fifteen feet above the stern of the boat coming straight at us.

"John, look out for that wave coming up behind us."

"Cappy, it ain't no different than any of the others we've had for the past four hours."

As he spoke, the mountain disappeared under the stern, which rose up like the last car on a roller coaster. It went under the stern with the wall of water so close that if the dinghy were hanging there, the first wave would have removed it for good. With our new, lofty, but brief perch on top of each wave, I could look past the stern and see a literal mountain range for miles around us. They were all between fifteen and twenty feet tall, breaking crests on about every tenth wave or so. The boat was no longer rolling. It was surfing down the face of the waves just as a surfer would. The hull speed would accelerate to over fifteen knots when making its flat out slide down the front of these huge waves. Amazingly, she seemed to be stable and controllable. I guess the question now was, could we remain stable and under control. John looked at me.

"I'm spent, Cappy. Can you take her for at least a couple hours?"

"You're damn right, John Silver. This is what I came for. I'll do it. You go below and get some rest."

"Just remember, Cappy, don't let her turn broadsides to a

wave, not even once. If she broaches and slides sideways down one of these monsters, well, it would be bad. Keep her at a slight angle down the face of each wave, just like a surfboard."

"I'll be careful John. Now get some rest."

Essie came topsides with a small glass of ginger ale and four pieces of toast with jelly on them.

"Here, Cappy, see if this will stick with you. If you want more, I'll fix it for you. I'm going to try and stay awake at least a couple more hours to see if you're OK."

"Thanks, Essie. I think I'm going to be all right now. The motion is a lot different and it doesn't seem to be bothering me as much. But, if you can, give me an hour or so and then you crash too."

Essie came up and sat beside me in the large cockpit of Calypso. I had always known that these old Pearsons had a good reputation and I had been impressed with how well she had done in the protected coastal areas I sailed her in. But now, I was really getting a new, larger dose of admiration for her. She was actually sailing, under full control, in literally gale conditions in the Atlantic. This possibility had to have been in the designer's mind when he drew her lines. At some point, at some time, he knew this would occur and he wanted his boat to be up to the test. All I could think was, this is really something. I looked up at the sails, just now realizing that the main had been totally furled and John Silver had apparently run up the storm trysail off the mast. Coupled with a storm staysail, we had up almost nothing and were still running at a tremendous speed.

"When did John put up the trysail, Essie?"

"He didn't, I put it up about three this morning. When the wind speed indicator started showing thirty-five knots, and the seas got so large, I knew I couldn't hold her into the seas safely while John went forward. Ten degrees too much either way and we'd fall off a wave and he'd be gone, so he held her for me and I ran up the sail. No big deal."

"I think you underestimate that, Essie. I don't think I could have gone out on that deck in the dark in these seas and done that. I really don't think so."

"Yeah, you could. You just haven't had to yet. You're next!"

The visual of this smallish woman doing that would stay in my mind for a long time.

"Look Essie, I'm fine. Go down and get some rest. If I need anything, I'll ring the ship's bell."

"You sure?"

"Absolutely. Get to bed."

Essie turned and took her worn out body below for what had to be a very needed sleep. I looked at the GPS. It was showing Charleston as still ninety-three miles away. We were making fabulous time, but could we outrun the fury of the full nor'easter headed this way? A serious one could have sustained winds of over seventy miles an hour for several days. The truth of it was, mariners realized that nor'easters sank far more ships and did more coastal damage than most hurricanes. Their average wind speed may be lower than a hurricane, but their duration wound up causing tons of damage. I knew that if the waves were already this tall and the wind was just over forty knots, I didn't want to see anything close to seventy knots. We needed this thing to hold off just through the night till after lunch tomorrow. We could make Charleston by one PM.

It's amazing to me to realize that you can get used to looking around a small boat in the ocean and seeing waves over twenty feet tall and thinking,

"this is fine, we're doing real well."

I wanted to handle things by myself as long as I possibly could. I knew that the enemy of sailors in these conditions was exhaustion. I had been there last night and John and Essie had stayed awake all night beyond me. The noise of the wind was beyond description. I could hear the whine of the rigging as the wind roared past it. The crashing of waves added to this made the sound level somewhere off the chart. We weren't within site of land and actually that was good news. The last place a boat should be in weather like this is close to shore. The waves are far worse in shallow water. It was going to be tricky to head into Charleston Inlet tomorrow if this got any worse. It would have to be a well thought out approach. The GPS put us about fifteen miles offshore. Thank God we were south of Cape Fear and all the shoals that dotted the coast above that. They would necessitate going much further offshore to clear them and that put you much closer to the northerly flowing Gulfstream. With four to five knots of current pushing the great Stream towards the north, impacting with the surface winds blowing to the south, phenomenally steep breaking seas would quickly develop. This had been the historically proven scenario of why you don't want to be out there with a northern wind. That's where the title Graveyard of the Atlantic came from. We were able to stay inshore enough to avoid the worst of that possibility. Anything worse than this, would be more than I wanted to see. We don't always get what we wish for.

By three PM, I could hear no stirring below. They had

collapsed into a coma apparently. I held off asking for help as long as I could. The temperature had dropped dramatically and the wind was building again. This had to be the leading edge of the nor'easter. It was to the point that all the sails needed to come off and possibly a warp or a drogue needed to be put out behind us to slow down our speed. Calypso was racing down the face of what were now twenty foot plus seas at such a pace that I was afraid we would submarine into the back of the next wave. We needed to be under better control. With great hesitancy, I rang the bell. John showed up first, still wearing his foul weather gear, hair uncombed and somewhat dumbfounded.

"What's the problem, Cappy? I'm almost awake."

"We have to slow her down, John. We've got to get down all the sails and possibly put out a warp or drogue. If you'll take the wheel, I'll go forward."

"You don't have to do that, Cappy, I'll go..."

"Nope, it's my turn. You ready to take the wheel?"

"Give me two minutes to get my cap on and rub the sleep out of my eyes."

No sooner did John appear on deck than did Essie, right behind him. She didn't need any explanation. I hooked my harness tether onto the deck-mounted nylon strap and inched forward. The overall motion was not as bad as the steep, quick pounding we had when we worked with the dinghy going to Ocracoke. I was more afraid of a huge wave washing across the deck trying to rip me off. I moved in spurts, trying to coordinate my movements with the movement of the boat. When it appeared that I had a stable five seconds coming up, I would undertake exactly five seconds worth of forward progress. I made it to the mast. Just as I arrived at that destination, a twenty-five footer went under us and I hugged the large aluminum tree with both hands as she plummeted down the almost vertical face. What a friggin' ride! No other adrenaline rush in my entire life compared to the one I was experiencing. There's nothing quite like a physical challenge where, if you lose, you die. The second we cleared the wave, our speed slowed again for the moment. I grabbed the halyard going to the top of the postage stamp of a main sail and fought with the small pin in the clevis for what seemed like two hours. Finally it cleared, just in time for me to hold the halyard and cling to the mast again for another wild ride. This wave was cresting and washed completely over the deck with about six inches of white and green water. I knew I couldn't let go of the halyard. There would be no way to retrieve it and it would flail in the rigging till something broke. I hung on for life. With the next lull, I took the clevis, secured it into the spinnaker mounting ring on the mast and then slid the base of the sail off the track. I took the bundled sail in my arms just as I saw the next wave approaching. With my arms full, there would be no way to hold me and the sail on deck and I didn't want to test the tensile strength of my harness tether. I did the only thing possible to my mind. In two giant leaps, I made it back to the cockpit. Essie had the side curtain pushed open and waiting. I literally threw the sail in and dove in behind it. Thank God, I didn't cover John with the sail. Steering blind would not have been good.

"Well that's half of it, now I just need to get in the storm staysail and we're done. Let me catch my breath."

It would have been very easy to just remain there, enjoying the false security afforded by the thin pieces of clear vinyl that made up the enclosure. Any one of the waves, if it washed just right across the deck could remove it. John understood that only too well. He had installed all of the companionway slats sealing off the interior of Calypso from any large wave that might poop the cockpit. I knew what had to be done. The trip forward needed to begin. I sucked it in as I said to Essie,

"Wasn't Dennis Hopper a great guy? I was really impressed. Just like a regular person. Well, I better go do this before I piss in my pants. Wish me luck."

"You can do it, Cappy, I'll hold her steady for you."

All of their assurances and positive remarks couldn't hide the concern in their faces. Not wanting to see anymore, it was best to just go do what must be done. I inched back out of the enclosure and repeated the trip forward. You know how you always hear that the more times you do something, the easier it gets? That does not apply in this situation. This could better be summed up by a saying that went, if I ever have to do this again, I'll throw up in my shoes. Now I knew what fun this would be. It took two deck drops, where I clung to the handrails on the cabin top as sections of the Blue Ridge Mountains zoomed by underneath, to get back to the for'deck. I grabbed the small sail, which felt like a piece of steel with all the wind it carried. I nodded to Essie who gave me a couple feet of slack in the halyard as it was tied off in the cockpit. I had to fight the clevis again for what seemed like hours and just for a second wondered why something like a snap wasn't used on these stupid things. Make a note; put stainless quick release halyard snaps on both sails. I secured the clevis alongside the first. Instead of removing the sail, I took a six-foot section of quarter inch line and wrapped it around the boom on the bottom of the staysail. The staysail was clubfooted, though the headsail was loose footed. Clubfooted means, there is a wooden or aluminum pole used at the bottom of the sail to secure it to. I don't know what knots I used to secure the sail. Nothing of quality came to mind. I remembered what one of my oldest sailing buddies, Charlie Hoefle used to tell me,

"Les, if you don't know any good knots, just use lots of 'em."

I always found that good advice and it truly seemed to apply here. It would undoubtedly take hours on deck in calm weather to get this mess off, but the sail was down and I didn't have to carry it in my arms back to the cockpit like a medic taking a wounded soldier on his back as he ran through a mine-field. This time, when I made it back, I laid on the cockpit floor for about fifteen minutes till I caught my breath. As I started to calm back down, I noticed that I was totally and completely drenched. This seemed remarkable in light of the fact that I was wearing very expensive foul weather gear bought with the specific intention of staying dry while sailing in bad weather. I guess making foul weather gear is like selling tornado shoes. The chances of someone actually getting the opportunity to test them by being sucked into a tornado precludes the amount of complaints that might actually come rolling in. Yet, folks living in tornado alley would all want a pair of them if they thought they would help at all.

"Don't get sucked up in a funnel cloud without the new, improved, Force Five Twisters! Three hundred fifty bucks a pair. Warranty void if used in areas of extreme low pressure."

I'm obviously kidding here, but if a foul weather gear manufacturer reads this....well don't be surprised if they use my add idea. I looked over at John and Essie. I could see the combination of relief that I was still alive and the sails were down coupled with increasing concern over our worsening situation. John broke the ice.

"Nice job, Cappy. We've slowed to a more manageable speed. Other than throwing out a warp, there's not much more we can do 'cept steer her real careful like. Essie, why don't you go below, and raise the Coast Guard on sixteen if you can. Tell 'em our situation, give 'em our position and tell 'em we'll check in with them every hour on the hour till we make port or this weather breaks. Just to be safe."

That was another very good idea. My crew was impressing me more by the second. I couldn't be out here under these conditions with anyone I would trust more than these two. I sat down by John Silver and we surveyed the view all around us. Surreal is the only term to describe what we saw. You could not adequately describe this to someone who had never been out here. Films, television, books, photos, none of those can realistically describe the scale and scope of a storm like this. We had done everything we could to help Calypso, now, she would have to do the hard work on her own. Her rigging, hull strength, and design characteristics were getting the ultimate field test. So far, she was meeting every challenge.

Essie reappeared from below.

"I was able to get a station at Murrell's Inlet, near Myrtle Beach. They were very concerned with our situation and said to not wait till things were desperate before we decided to get picked up. In other words, when the boat is sinking or one of us is in the water. I guess that would be desperate enough. What do you guys think we should do? Les, it's your boat. Will she make it?"

"I will say without hesitation that I believe if we can make it, Calypso will be fine. She is sound. I just had her surveyed for insurance last year and the guy told me she was built like a cinderblock with a sail on it. If you're frightened, I understand, and we'll evacuate, get airlifted out of here. But, my vote is to ride it out. We only have to make it about fourteen more hours and we're still moving south like a rocket."

Essie looked at John.

"And you, John?"

"I guess I'll stay right here with Cappy. It ain't often a sailor gets to test themselves like this. I ain't got no better place to be. We're going to make it."

Night began to fall early. The sky was already so dark that it needed very little help to suppress any remaining light. As hard as it had been to steer precisely down the face of seas we could see, it was a far different matter to accomplish that feat at night, a very pitch black night. I was at the wheel. John was taking the first nap tonight and we would all be taking shifts. We decided that no one should be on watch alone. We could use staggered shifts so that one person would sleep three hours and there would always be two awake. I was thankful that I had all day to get used to steering the boat down the waves while they were visible. I knew what I needed to do now; I just needed to figure out the when without seeing the waves. I soon realized that I could tell as much from wave sounds and the time between waves as I needed to know. I now knew what it must feel like for a blind person to ride a roller coaster. In some ways it was easier. I couldn't see the waves coming or how bad things were all around me. There was just one nagging thought in the back of my mind. I knew that in any storm such as this, that periodically, even though all of the waves were huge, a rogue wave could appear that was up to sixty percent larger than the average. With an average here of around twenty-five feet, that would mean a wave could come through up to forty-five, maybe fifty feet tall. A slide down the face of one of those could be beyond recovering from. I felt my rectum pucker at just the thought. The visual was like hanging over the edge of the Grand Canyon, looking down at the Colorado River while someone held the back of my belt to keep me from going over. It's a feeling I never liked.

Throughout the night, things remained constant. The shift changes worked as we planned and no one became too exhausted. We managed to grab small bites of food between shifts though something warm, like coffee, or soup and a grilled cheese sandwich would have been worth a King's ransom. As dawn came slowly and made its presence known, we were all awake. We knew we were closing in on Charleston and if we could just hang on a little longer we would be safe. Essie had now made contact with the Coast Guard unit there and we had seen a chopper fly over at first light. He circled us, and raised us on the VHF.

"Sailing vessel, Calypso, Calypso, this is Coast Guard unit Charleston, Air Rescue Two overhead. We have visual contact with you. What is your present situation? Are you in need of assistance at this time?"

We all knew the answer to that one. We were within four hours of harbor and we wouldn't be deserting this great little ship that had carried us so far.

"Coast Guard Air Rescue Charleston, this is Calypso, negative. We are under control, the crew is well and we anticipate reaching Charleston Harbor within four hours. We appreciate your concern and request Charleston to monitor our progress."

"Affirmative, Calypso. Please maintain your hourly reports and make contact if you need additional help. Coast Guard

Charleston Sea Rescue Two, out."

It did feel good to know we were less than a ten-minute helicopter flight out of Charleston and they found us very easily which is not as simple a task as they made it look. Anticipation of an end to this nightmare was building.

The waves were still very large. They were consistent and predictable for the most part and our strategy for handling them had served us very well. We now needed to change course and begin a very slight turn towards shore. Otherwise, we would be fifteen miles directly offshore from Charleston and there is no way we could run in broadside to these waves. A broach would occur very quickly.

"John, we need to start heading in slowly. From the looks of things, I'd suggest about ten degrees to starboard. That will get us in before we get to the ship channel. We don't want to go past it or have to turn broadside to the waves."

"Sounds good to me, Cappy. Ten degrees it is."

We were all a little antsy about change of any kind that would alter the workable motion we had found. However, we were not in the full bore of the storm yet. This nor'easter could get far worse, to the point that Coast Guard assistance might be next to impossible and we needed to be in port, ASAP. The course change slowed our run down the face of the waves slightly, but extended the length of the ride and the roll at the end of the ride since the crest ran under more of the side of the boat than the stern. This was going to be tricky. We would be on an angle that was somewhere between the manageable angle we had been on and broadside, the possible broach angle. Intense concentration on the wheel was needed and the prospect of an immediate turn to port if a roll even seemed to be getting started. This was scary stuff.

The first hour went by like a week. We were now eleven miles out according to the GPS. Our strategy was working. As we continued to inch towards shore, the waves became noticeably more erratic and steeper. There was more whitewater around us. All the sleazy attorneys in the kingdom couldn't make this whitewater go away. As we approached the end of the second hour, our worst fear became reality. We actually saw it coming.

"Oh shit, John, Essie, look behind us!"

Moving up quickly, now about the fourth wave back was the friggin' granddaddy of all the waves we had seen over the past two days. My first thought was to round it off,

"fifty foot at least, and cresting. Head port, head port, take it more on the stern."

There was no fear on John or Essie's face. Concern, intense concentration, but no fear. I hoped they couldn't read it on my mine. It was certainly inside.

"I'll hold her, Cappy, we'll ride her."

Calypso swung to port and the waves preceding the giant went under us just like all the ones we'd already rode. Then it was here. I sucked in a large gulp of air and for some reason began to hold my breath. A huge, absolutely monstrous, practically vertical wall of water was about twenty feet behind us and ready to ride us, not the reverse. I looked at John's hands on the wheel; they were as white knuckled as they could get. He had practically squeezed all the blood out of them. Then the incredible lifting motion began. We were in the Shuttle, leaving Canaveral, heading straight up and even more up, God when will we reach the top of this thing? And then, the blast forward started. At a speed I can't even estimate, it felt like about fifty miles an hour, we began to rush down the face of this thing. Talk was not possible, the noise was deafening. I saw John make slight turns back to starboard to try and get a small angle on the wave. He knew we didn't want to take a straight dive down the face of this wall. All I could think of was, God, please don't let us turtle, don't roll baby, please stay upright. I looked back towards the crest of the wave and saw the massive cloud of frothing white, like the head of a beer the size of Lake Michigan. John saw it too and increased our turn slightly more to starboard. We were perilously close to our point of no return, an angle we couldn't right ourselves from. As we continued at this light speed pace, we began to move away from the white water. As I looked back, the top of the wave where we had just been collapsed on to the wall below it forming a tube the size of the Towne Mountain tunnel in Asheville. You could have driven eighteen wheelers through it. But, the water under us was not white. As the tip of the mountain went under us, we slowed quickly, our bow raised and then we began to recede down the back of this great giant. Essie looked at me.

"Please tell me there's not another back there."

I looked to stern; the rest were still big but not like what we had just experienced.

"I think we have all just ridden a rogue, Essie. John, for crying out loud, that was masterful. You couldn't have done it any better, I mean like a friggin' surgeon. Holy crap! We made it!"

"Well, Cappy, we're still a good ten miles out and we ain't even in the middle of the nor'easter. We need to get the hell out of here, now."

We counted every wave, photographed them in our minds

and compared them to the one we all had enlarged in our memory's thirty-second film processing center so recently. No reprints would ever be needed. After two hours, and two more fly-overs by the Sea Rescue chopper, they contacted us on the radio.

"Calypso, the number one sea buoy is approximately two miles ahead of you and will require a fifteen degree correction to port to align properly."

Our strategy had worked. We were coming in slightly ahead of the channel allowing us to run with the waves to the marker and not sideways to them.

"I'm going to fire up the diesel, we're going to need to motor soon to stay in the center of the channel. Please start, please."

That was wasted aggravation. I turned the key, hit the glow plug for fifteen seconds and then the starter button. The old Perkins cranked like it had been sitting in a warm harbor for two days. Relief spread among us.

As we made good the number one buoy, we all knew one last obstacle was ahead. The waves on either side of the channel were breaking like skyscrapers falling over. The channel was about a tenth of a mile wide this far out but very shallow on either side of it. The huge waves running down the coast were meeting the bottom here with great amounts of unhappiness. We literally could not see a buoy till we were almost on them and striking one would be a bad ending to an otherwise miraculous tale. From a short distance away, they appeared to be tiny floating bobbers like you would use with a bamboo fishing pole. Once you were close, you could see they were really huge, metal cans, held to the bottom with massive chains attached to God only knows what kind of anchors they must require. Striking one would split us apart instantly. We just couldn't see them. We were flying blind, looking for the calm water while staring at a small chart of the harbor channel. I quickly took an angle from the chart that I felt would be close but I knew that we were still going to need just plain old luck to stay in the channel without seeing the buoys. I kept having flashbacks to the picture in Cruising World of the Morning Dew, her busted hull on the jetty here at dawn, the morning after she struck the rocks and all her crew was lost. Yes, there IS a rock jetty to the side of the channel here. I didn't think we could be sure that we were in the channel. Fear was really building. I could see it in John and Essie's faces. Had we gone through all this just to wind up on the rocks? Seconds were ticking by and we were moving quickly towards the next marker. It had to be getting close. It was taking too long. Had we passed it? Were we out of the channel? Was the jetty coming up quickly? We could now make out the shoreline, water tanks and buildings clearly, but they were all above the boiling furor we were a part of right now. I mentally braced for impact. Essie heard it first.

"Calypso, Calypso, this is Coast Guard Group Charleston. We are approaching in a cutter at two o'clock, just off your starboard. Do you see us? We have you on radar."

And there they were, like the angel on top of the Christmas tree, this beautiful white, forty-four foot cutter with its bold orange stripe. They were coming to show us the way home!

"Calypso, we are going to do a one-eighty here between the next two waves, do you have enough power to follow us?"

"Affirmative, Coast Guard. Just lead the way."

We made the twenty-degree correction to starboard and gave the old diesel some fuel. The rolling was back but it was to be short lived. After about thirty seconds, I swallowed hard when I saw the large green sea buoy to our port side. Before the correction, we would have come in at least a hundred yards to the outside of it, possibly enough to have ruined our day. It took almost an hour to make good the entrance. The huge swells began to die around us as we saw the city open up in front. Once inside, on the far calmer waters of the Cooper River, the Coast Guard waved us off and we thanked them profusely over the radio. They had been like an American Embassy flying the Stars and Stripes in a war zone. It is hard to describe the feeling of exhilaration that accompanies the successful completion of something so trying as this had been. Though luck, both good and bad, had played out their parts, good sailing and a tough old boat had a large amount to do with the outcome also.

The Real Calypso - A Gulfstar 43

Chapter Eight

I felt tired and ready for my feet to touch land. Essie looked over at me.

"Les, how would you feel about me paying for a slip tonight? I want to take a hot shower in a big bathroom and go to a burger joint or something instead of cooking. I'll treat you there too if need be. What do you say?"

"Essie, there is no way I'd let my crew pay for anything tonight. I haven't visited here before by boat, but we'll pick a marina out of the cruising guide and do just what you said. I'd like to feel a little terra firma myself."

I grabbed the coastal cruising guide to the South Atlantic region, picked out nearby Young's Yacht Service and Marina and gave the directions to John. Within minutes we had located a new facility, not far past the famous Charleston Battery. I could see the 'I want to look around Charleston' look on Essie's face. She could pretty well have whatever she wanted after her performance the past two days. John could also, for that matter. The dockmaster met us and directed us to a floating slip. He was a young, friendly sort, maybe sixteen years old.

"That was you guys we heard the Coast Guard talking with all morning?"

"I'm afraid so, son. You could hear it clearly in here?"

"Well, we could hear the Coast Guard's part of it and then yours too, about an hour ago. It was right tense to even listen to. How bad is it out there?"

"On a scale of one to ten, it's been about a fifteen for the past twenty-four hours. If anybody ever asks you about 'going for it' when it's like this, don't. Just say no, as the poster says. You couldn't beat me enough to get me to go back offshore in this. I was surprised the Coast Guard was even willing to do it for us."

"Aw, those guys love it. They practice here at the inlet every time there's a storm. I've seen 'em go out when it's a lot worse than this."

"Well, it won't be to come help us, that's for sure. I think we've just been through the worst storm we're ever going to sail in."

"It's supposed to blow like Hell here tonight. You know, there's a nor'easter building?"

"Yeah, we definitely know. Where's the showers?"

"Right around the corner. Combination is four, three, one."

"Is there a decent place close by to get a burger and a beer?"

"That would be the Battery Tavern, two blocks down on the right. Big screen TV, pool tables and most of the locals. I'll be there after I get off work. All the fine young women hang there."

"Thanks, by the way, what's your name?"

"Stephen. My sister Shannon and I actually run the place for our Uncle John. He and Aunt Sami don't like hanging out here. They're pretty much retired and just hang out on their boat, the Aletha B. It's down at the end of the pier. You'll meet them tomorrow. He was listening to the radio real close this morning, to hear what was going on with you guys. I know he'll want to hear all about it."

"Let us get cleaned up, some chow and some rest and to-morrow we'll retell the tale. Besides, that will give us all some time to even make the story more exciting, if that's possible."

"Yes sir, see you later."

After we got the boat secured, hosed the salt off her and got the electricity hooked up to shore power, we grabbed our duf-fel bags and limped up to the showers. Speaking for the group, I think I would be safe in saying that it was the singular best shower any of us had ever taken. I didn't know whether it was because it actually felt that good or whether if it was the relief I was feeling at being able to be anywhere after such a close ride with eternity. I stayed in the steaming water for at least twenty full minutes. My fingers had started to shrivel when I got out. I actually shaved, brushed my teeth, dried my hair and even put on some Old Spice after-shave. I would never use that at work, but on the boat, I loved the old bottle with the sailboat on it. It felt right. I carried my dirty clothes and wet towel back to the boat. We could find a laundry tomorrow. I was sure everyone would be on board waiting for me. Wrong, I waited for them for another twenty minutes. Apparently, it felt just as good to them. When you're cruising, a hot shower can be one of life's small treasures. As I watched them come down the dock together, I was glad they were along with me. In their own way, both had added immeas-urably to the trip and to my world in general. I really liked them both. I was especially being attracted to the dark haired, strong-minded young woman who came along just to be our ship's cook. She was far more than that.

The wind was howling like mad outside and the clanging of sailboat halyards was like a chorus of steelworkers banging with hammers on a sheet metal wall. No matter, to us, it was a calm evening. The ground under our feet was not rising and falling twenty feet every five seconds.

The Battery Tavern was hopping. It was like many other places in the historical section of the city. It looked more like a colonial tavern than a modern big city bar. But, the patrons gave it away. They were a hardy mix of young and old, many watching the South Carolina gamecocks loose to N.C State University, upsetting their evening, but not nearly so much as it was for Coach Lou Holtz. I was particularly delighted, but wise enough to keep it to myself. We got a seat near the window and could look out on the harbor we were so grateful to make. A sizeable group was at a nearby table and their laughter reminded me of my own circle of friends that would be celebrating weekends without me, at out favorite watering holes in New Bern. I was drawn to their laughter. An older, distinguished looking, white haired guy at the head of the table saw I was looking their way. He motioned towards me and the waiter came over.

"Mr. Young wants to know if your group would like to join their party. He said you looked like sailors."

"We are."

"He can always pick them out. You probably walked up here from his marina."

"Oh, he's the guy who owns Young's Yacht Service?"

"That's him, and the pretty blonde lady beside him is his wife, Sami. You'll like them."

We walked over to the group who had already pulled up three chairs for us. His wife, smiling ear to ear, said,

"Hi, I'm Sami. I'm just telling a story on John, sit down. You'll love it, this is funny as Hell."

We sat down as she continued.

"So, John decided to try Viagra. But, it was late and he was tired. I came back in from the bathroom, looking good, smelling great, new negligee and find John, snoring his nose off. However, the wonder drug had done it stuff. He was at full attention. I slept under a tent all night."

By now the group was busting out with laughter, John was sitting by just smiling at the way his wife was telling the story.

"and, in the morning when I woke up, John was still snoring, the tent was still up and the cat had crawled up on the bed and was swatting at his manhood like a scratch pole!"

She gestured a pawing motion, as the cat would have been making. It was riotously funny, and told by a professional. These were definitely sailors.

John and Sami Bills

We quickly became an integral part of the evening's festivities. Once John and Sami realized we were the boat out in the storm, we were asked to relate the events from start to finish. I came to realize that finally, after a half of a century on the planet, I had a real life tale that would require absolutely no 'beefing up' to be completely mesmerizing when telling others. God, I had always wanted one of those. It was also apparent that when in a group with John and Essie, we would have to decide who had the best perspective on a particular aspect of the tale and assign it to them permanently, much like casting a play. I could see the terror in the group's eyes when we joined chorus to render the part about the giant wave that we rode for so long. Man, this was fun. However, the reality of it was, we were far more exhausted than anyone else present, so we dismissed ourselves as we needed to be asleep immediately. The three of us walked abreast down the old cobbled sidewalk, Essie in the middle, arms around each other's shoulders, back to Calypso. We were completely content with the world that evening. However, morning would bring about some new developments in our cruise that would be very perplexing.

Young's Marina was a very busy place. The kids that basically ran the place, Shannon, or Shanny as everyone called her and Stephen were very cheerful and I couldn't help but think how much I would have enjoyed working somewhere like this when I was a kid. I'd probably still be there. I was up very early and feeling completely recharged though a little sore from all the pounding the previous day. Calypso was disheveled and I figured we would need to stay in Charleston at least a day or two before heading South again. Besides, Charleston fell within the parameters of places I was willing to spend time. My general rule is, 'if palm trees won't grow there, I don't want to go there.' There were lots of palms around here, both natural and planted. The charm of the old South was also evident everywhere you looked. There were old southern homes, which had overlooked Charleston Harbor since before the Civil War, narrow streets, Savannah style steps and porches winding into alleys between the houses and wonderful restaurants. Charming taverns and gift shops all maintained the look and feel that made Charleston special.

Shannon and Stephen in Charleston

It was certainly a favorite of sailors. All of this was within easy walking distance of the marina.

Since breakfast is the best bang for the buck, we decided to walk downtown to a small cafe that Shanny had suggested and pig out. We could cook aboard the rest of the day after we got

Calypso straightened out. We were about a hundred yards from the boat when I realized that I had brought no money with me.

"You guys go ahead, I'm going to run back to Calypso and get a little cash."

Essie and John both offered to spring for my breakfast, but I felt it was best that I paid my own way most of the time. My God, I wasn't paying them anything to crew, the least I could do was occasionally buy a meal, and breakfast was the cheapest meal of the day. They relented and I jogged back to Calypso. I rummaged around on the shelf over my berth till I found the cash jar, lying on its side on the back corner where it had come to rest after yesterday's constant rolling. I knew that, between what food and drinks had been bought and topping off the diesel tank that I had to have whittled the four hundred bucks down to about two fifty. I had purposely avoided looking into the jar as much as possible as it would always slam home the reality to me that I didn't have any money and this cruise was living on borrowed time. I had no clue what I would do when I went to the jar and it was finally empty. I'd probably have to tell Essie and John that the dream had come to an abrupt end and that I would have to stay wherever we where and pump gas till I got enough money to head out again. Oh well, I still had a few bucks and I'd just make it last as long as possible. As Scarlet O'Hara once said, "tomorrow's another day". I unscrewed the jar and was more than a little confused to find that it was not growing empty, in fact, it was jammed completely full. I poured the contents out on my bunk and counted out, "two hundred, four hundred, five, seven", winding up with an even thousand bucks.

"What the Hell?"

I felt a heavy weight being lifted off my shoulders and at

the same time, the overpowering question,

"Who would have done this? Essie? John?"

I didn't really think it could be either of them knowing that they were in just as bad a shape financially as I was, though both had shown generosity and the desire for this trip to keep going. The only possible explanation was Melinda Katz. She must have had the cleaning crew put the money in here while we were being driven around town. But why? Why did she have such an interest in Calypso, or me? I know we had a brief romantic evening together, and as wonderful as it was, I didn't think it was life altering for either of us and I would have second thoughts about doing anything like that again. Face it, I had been a monk in a passionless relationship for years and was an explosion waiting to happen. And now, it was all a little embarrassing to me, especially around Essie. I was very much attracted to and interested in her. I was hoping that there were some of those same feelings in her. I had made up my mind I would be friendly with Melinda if she came on to me in any fashion, but that would be the extent of it from my point. She couldn't be that caught up in me. I mean, sure, I was in reasonably good condition for slightly into extended middle age. Some women are actually attracted to balding men and the glasses, well they speak volumes about intellectualism, am I correct? But, the cleaning crew was the only folks who had been onboard since we left Ocracoke and I had gotten money out of the jar since then. I would most definitely have noticed if there had been a significant increase of money in there. Did Melinda just feel sorry for me? True, a thousand bucks to her would probably be more like leaving a tip to a waiter after great service, but, if that is what she was doing here, it, well, it just made me feel kinda' cheap. But, I was going to share my good fortune with Essie and John, and God only knows I needed the money. So, I resolved to just shut up about it, and see what happened from here on out. The chances of running into the Katz Meow again were almost nil since she cruised at about twelve knots and we were only averaging five or six. I would just consider this an instance of incredibly good fortune; something my life had not been too full of previously. I took out one of the crisp, new hundred dollar bills, closed up Calypso and headed downtown to catch up with my crew.

I walked into the Palm Room grill just as the waitress was bringing coffee to Essie and John. John motioned me over.

"We already got your coffee coming. Neat place, huh? Knew you'd love the name with your fondness for Palm Trees. The jukebox has every Buffett song he ever recorded. I'll bet this place is really hopping in the evening."

It seemed that every restaurant in Charleston was half restaurant half bar. That worked just fine for the crew of Calypso.

"Thanks. Well guys, eat up, breakfast is on me."

Essie looked over at me.

"You know you don't have to buy breakfast for us. I brought a little money along and I don't mind sharing what I have."

"Hey, no problem. I found a little extra cash in the boat I didn't know I had. Must have left it there a while back and just forgot about it. We'll make it to the Bahamas now, if there's no unforeseen problems."

"Alright then, Cappy!" exclaimed John.

"This trip was just meant to be. I could feel it the night I met you in Captain Ratty's. I learned a long time ago to just go with my gut feelings. Always works out somehow."

We lingered at breakfast, told a bunch of great sailing stories. I even got that warm fuzzy feeling I was particularly fond of when describing my last day at Carolina Bible Corp. I think that will always be one of my favorites. I was fighting a losing battle to stop myself from embellishing it each time I retold it. I wanted to remember that moment forever just as it happened. It was a moment of Biblical proportions, something akin to Moses leading his people to the Promised Land.

We walked back towards the marina, stopping to look at every single palm tree. God, what they did to my psyche. I don't know what exactly the effect they caused was, but I felt ten degrees warmer just looking at one. We walked slowly and enjoyed the moment. As we approached the harbor, we could see several boats entering, what a beautiful sight they are. John brought me back to the real world.

"Cappy, I think it wouldn't be a bad idea to change out the oil and fuel filters about now. If we're gonna' stay inside till we hit Florida, which I highly recommend based on these nor'easters sliding past here every few days, we're gonna' be motoring quite a bit and wouldn't hurt to know we got everything clean in the motor. I'm willing to bet'cha we stirred up a lot of crap in the fuel tank with all that banging around. If a filter is gonna' clog, this would be the time."

"OK, John I'll help you accomplish that little task."

"No need, Cappy. There's not much room around the engine; we'd just be in each other's way. Why don't you look around the docks a little while I knock this out? Won't take long."

"You have twisted my arm, John Silver. Essie, want to come with me?"

"I'd love to do just that."

We started making the rounds of the marina. I don't know what it is, but sailors never tire of looking at sailboats. They are art to me, the perfect combination of form and function. Sailors will always tell you that when you are looking to buy a boat, the right one will almost speak to you when you board her, much like a dog in a pet store. You'll just know that you've found the right one. It's also said that when you find the right boat, every time you leave her, you'll always take just one last look back, much like leaving a woman you love. Since I was about ten years old, nothing had ever beat just walking around a marina looking at boats. I noticed that Essie had the same predilection. She pointed out which ones caught her eye and then proceeded to explain what it was about a certain boat, its sheer, its coach roof, the rig, whatever it was that she liked about it. She knew a lot about sailboats. She could tell a ketch from a schooner or a yawl, a cutter from a sloop, a heavy displacement hull from a centerboarder and all the other little nuances that let me know she knew what she was talking about. All this and she was still a very lovely woman. She didn't need make-up or tight fitting clothes to be attractive. She had a smile that would light up a city block at night and eyes that sparkled more than the ocean with the sun beating down on it. I just wanted to put my arm around her. As we walked along, I finally mustered up my nerve and grabbed her hand. What's the worst she could do? Tell me that it was just not wanted? I was willing to risk it. It was thrilling when she didn't pull away but rather, squeezed my hand just enough to let me know she wanted it there. This was a wondrous sign and the sky seemed to brighten about fifty percent with this turn of events. We took our time, walking down every finger pier, talking with anyone that seemed chatty and even accepting invitations to come aboard several boats. We finally made our way back to Calypso where a greasy, irritated looking John Silver awaited us.

"Bad news, Cappy. We've got some engine problems."

I really didn't need to hear that. Repairs to a diesel can add up quick, fast, and in a hurry.

"What's the problem? Anything we can fix ourselves?"

"There's water in one of the cylinders. We've either got a crack in the block or an exhaust backup. Even if I can repair it, which I'm not really sure I can do, it's going to involve taking the head off, checking the cylinder, a new gasket set, a few tools we don't have, like a torque wrench to put the head back on and a few other things. You'll be lucky if we can do this ourselves and get away for under five boat units. A boat unit is the somewhat unendearing term boat-owner's use for a hundred bucks. Almost nothing for a boat costs less than one boat unit. All I could think off was, "thank God, that money was put in the money jar or we would be coming to a screeching end of this cruise, right here in Charleston.

"Well, John. Let's go at it. I can put the parts on my charge card up to five hundred bucks. If it's over that, I still have a little cash. We've gotta' have the motor running to keep this cruise going. I certainly don't want to leave Charleston if it's less than perfect."

"OK, Cappy, I'll start breaking her down and drawing up a list of what we need. Might as well get the new filters for oil and fuel while we're doing it. Just keep your fingers crossed that it's not a cracked block. I don't think it could be, cause we haven't run her hot at all. I'll bet it was a back-fill through the exhaust. That would be the best scenario."

Six hours later, the engine room was a shambles. John and I were completely covered in grease. Between the two of us, we knew just enough about diesels to get in trouble. We had drawn a schematic as we went, labeling every part and making a note about where it came from. We were optimistic that we could clean the water out of the cylinder, lube it up, reassemble the head, bleed the lines and fire her up, no harm done. We did, however need to make a run to Palmetto Diesel in the industrial section of Charleston and pick up the needed parts. Shanny got John and Sami's car for us. I'm sure she asked permission, oh yeah, and off we went. It was just about five PM when we arrived but, the affable parts manager, Pat Tilson welcomed us like long lost suckers, I mean cousins.

"Tell you what, boys. It's getting late, but I'm gonna' stay right here till we get you all fixed up. By the way, how you paying for this? We take all major credit cards and of course, cash."

It was apparent he was used to dealing with cruising sailors, always broke and looking for a deal. After thinking about it for a minute, I came to a management decision. It would be better to save our cash for the places that wouldn't take credit cards and go ahead and put it on the credit card, as long as it wasn't over the five hundred-dollar limit. I handed Pat the card.

"Here, let's try this one."

After about twenty minutes, John was convinced we had enough junk to get the motor running and change all the filters and oil. Pat began to ring up the items. Without bothering to tell me the total, as I had asked, he ran the card. In only a second, the signature slip came out of the card box indicating it had been accepted. I was doubly relieved. That meant that the card was not only still good, but the amount was under the five hundred-dollar limit. I looked at the ticket before signing. I was shocked.

"Pat, this amount is six hundred and thirty five bucks. Jeez, that's a lot more than I was expecting, and it's considerably over the limit on this card."

"Hey man, parts cost what they cost, marine diesel parts ain't cheap. You know, I don't run a government operation here, we have to make a profit. And, they accepted the card just fine. You must have had a limit increase you forgot about."

Pat Tilson doesn't really run a parts store, but is a rascal.

I knew better than that. I signed the card, John grabbed the box of parts and we headed back to Calypso. I was pissed off about the cost, but I was at least glad we would have a thoroughly tuned motor by tomorrow and then we could move on. I was still four hundred bucks ahead of where I thought I was with the mysterious addition to the money jar. When we got back to the marina, I let John carry the parts on to the boat and I visited the payphone. I dialed the eight hundred number on my credit card to see if by some miracle my limit had been increased. Now, I don't want you to think I'm some kinda' moron, so here's as close as I can remember, the actual conversation.

"Thank you for calling, how can I help you?"

"Yes Mam, I just placed a sizable purchase on my credit card. I think it was slightly over my limit and yet it appeared to be accepted. Can you check this out for me?"

"Of course, Sir."

I gave her my name, rank and serial number as requested and she offered the following information.

"Sir, in checking your account, your purchase was valid in keeping with the terms of your card."

"I thought I had a five hundred dollar limit."

"The account was set up that way, Mr. Pendleton, but now that your card is backed by a draft account, the limit on your card has been increased to ten thousand dollars. The amount of actual advances will be drafted from your account each month and then start over. So, you're obviously way under your limit."

"Excuse me, but there has to be a mistake here. I've made no changes to my account since I got the card. What is the name on the bank account you're drafting?"

"It appears that it is a numbered account, Sir. I can confirm your number if you know it but I can't give you the number over the phone. Or, if you would like to write us at our Corporate Center, someone there might be able to help you. I'm sure that everything is fine, Sir. They always check out draft situations very carefully before authorizing limits this large. Can I help you with anything else today?"

"No thank you. I'm confused enough."

Now I really was shell-shocked. This made no friggin' sense to me at all. It was too much to be believed that Melinda Katz was doing this. OK, I think I'm pretty good in the sack, but nobody is this good. But, there was no other possible explanation. The card was in the cash jar with my money that suddenly tripled. The cleaning crew could have copied the number down and given it to her. I was needing to see Melinda Katz now, badly. If she was expecting something from me for this outpouring of generosity, I would have to set her straight, as much as I needed the cash. I did not want to travel with a feeling of growing indebtedness to someone I didn't even know. I guess the confusion was still on my face as I stepped below in Calypso. Essie could see it on my face.

"Les, what's wrong? Looks like you've seen a ghost."

"I'm fine. Just having a little problem with a credit card company. Something is really screwed up in my account. I tried to tell them it was wrong but they just don't want to hear it."

"Have they cut you off?"

"Just the opposite. They increased my card limit to an unbelievable amount without me even asking for it and there's not only no way I could pay it back, they've got somebody else's bank account number listed as the place to send the bill. Since I put more on the card today than what my limit was supposed to be, I think I'll just cut the card up so I won't get stuck with some huge bill next month."

John had a better idea.

"Look, why not just put the card away where you won't be tempted to use it and see if they don't get it straight. That way, God forbid, we have an emergency of some sort, you know, somebody gets hurt or something, you could put it on the card and worry about it later."

"That makes sense. That's what I'll do."

I decided to not mention the extra cash as that might begin to make me look borderline weird.

"Well, John. How does the motor situation look?"

"Cappy, things go half decent, we'll be running by lunch tomorrow."

"That's great news. Look, it's pretty dark out. Why don't we wash up a little and go get a beer?"

Essie jumped right on that one.

"Let's go, Les. Tonight, I'll buy the first round."

I hadn't told her, but I did like her calling me Les instead of Cappy or Skip. I kinda' got the feeling she liked saying my name. I certainly liked hearing her call my name.

We walked down the dock just in time to see two very familiar looking boats pulling in. They were from home. It was Ronnie and Connie Cousino and Eddy and Jennifer from back home. They had been to St. Augustine, Florida and we must have been catching them on the way home. Ronnie was a stockbroker and Eddy was a hotshot CPA from Raleigh. Would they ever be surprised to see me standing there to take their lines? This would be fun. I pulled my cap down over my face.

"Evening, Skipper. Throw me a bow line and I'll get you secure up here. Connie, aboard Memories tossed me a dock line.

I secured it and then made the same gesture to Jennifer on board their boat, Anticipation. I secured them both and then backed off a ways. These were both very high dollar yachts. Ronnie and Eddy were both fanatics about keeping them Bristol and they always looked like they just got them off the showroom floor. Of course, they were both high rollers of the first order, so it was a lot easier for them than for some of us a little less well heeled. They were both great couples though. We had spent many evenings together and nothing delighted me more than to put a spanking on Ronnie's high-speed sloop. Of course, that was something that only occurred in heavy weather since his boat was a light air rocket. We had a friendly rivalry going on between us. And Eddy Parker was a great guy who always just smiled in a good sport fashion when he was the butt of the relentless onslaught of lawyer jokes that made the rounds of our group. When he was looking for a name for his new Elite, one member of our group suggested the name Bottomfeeder. Eddy laughed as loud as anyone else and we all appreciated his willingness to laugh at himself. They were all good people. Ronnie stepped off first. I walked up to him, hat down low on my forehead and offered.

"Sir, as much as we'd like to offer you a slip here, we're just not going to able to do that, what with your unabashed willingness to travel with an attorney."

For a moment he was stunned. I was the last person he ever expected to see here.

"Les, you son of a gun. What the heck are you doing here?"
"Running away from home, headed to the Keys and maybe the Bahamas for the winter."

"Where's your family?"

"We are all going our separate ways if you get my meaning."

"I'm sorry, I hadn't heard."

"No problem. Things have been headed this way for a long time."

Captain Ron and First Mate Connie Cousino off "Memories"

Eddy and Jennifer walked up next and repeated the same questions to which I gave the same answers.

"By the way, let me introduce you to my crew. This is Essie and John Silver."

Essie shook hands with everyone but John Silver was no where to be found. I guessed he had gone back to Calypso.

"We're headed to the Battery Tavern for a beer. You folks like to join us?"

"You're on. Give us a few minutes to straighten up."

We walked as a group towards the slip where Calypso was moored. John Silver was nowhere to be found.

"Well, John knows where we're headed. He might have gone to the marina bathrooms. I'm sure he'll come in later."

We continued on to the Battery Tavern. The place was full this evening. We got a large table in front of the fireplace and instructed the waiter to prepare for the worst. Even though our group had now doubled, Essie still insisted on buying the first round. After several beers and more detailed information about the trip we were all in the middle of, the talk came around to one story that Ron Cousino hoped that someday he would outlive. It was about the incident that occurred to him several years prior that earned him the nickname Tampon Ron. The story, which I have been assured by more than one observer and participant was completely true, goes something like this.

Ronnie has a lot of anal tendencies when it comes to his boat; a boat I might add, which is sometimes slower than mine. It's a 1993 Hunter 37.5 Legend. The lengths that he goes to while keeping her Bristol are legendary. He actually paints the bilge twice a year, God's truth. Well, he apparently became concerned over a perceived dirt buildup in his sail track. I've already said, God's truth. Anyway, someone mentioned to him, or maybe he read it somewhere, he somehow came up with a unique solution. He would tie a tampon to the halyard, which normally raises the sail to the top of the mast, some fifty-five feet in the air. He tightly secured the tampon (super tampon, I'm told) to the halyard as he didn't want it to come loose half way up the mast. He then tied a small cord to the clevis on the halyard so that he could pull it back down once it reached the top of the mast. Thus secured, he began to raise and lower the tampon. However, there had been a quite heavy dew that morning and the sail slot in the mast was apparently wet. Stop, you're getting ahead of me. That's right, the tampon, predictably began to swell, more and more. Eventually, it became solidly wedged in the sail track, near the very top. He tried for quite some time, I'm told, before he was willing to confide in anyone exactly what the problem was. He eventually told his neighbor, a very attractive young woman named Donna, who always wore the skimpiest bikinis, about his dilemma. Between outbursts of laughter, which attracted a considerable number of people to the event, Donna hooked up a boson's chair to the spinnaker halyard and Ronnie managed to pull her up the mast, bikini and all. Ronnie embarrasses fairly quickly which made the scene all that much more memorable and worthy of reliving constantly. In a way, we all look at this as therapy for him. Later, at a party one very cold, beer fueled evening, two friends of ours wrote and sang the song TAMPON RON. It's a bluesy sort of thing with wonderful lyrics, kind of a sing-along where everyone takes a verse. It has made Captain Ron sort of a legend in our area. Essie roared with laughter over the story. Ronnie reciprocated by telling everyone about my most embarrassing moment. This was a rather insignificant event that occurred while I was installing a new teak and holly sole in a Pearson Coaster, a thirty foot sloop I had owned previously. I inadvertently drilled a hole through the bottom of the boat as it sat there in the water and that's really all that needs to be told here today. Essie loved that one even more than Tampon Ron for some reason.

The evening turned out to be a very good one, barring the absence of John Silver. I could only figure that he must not be feeling too well and turned in early. We, on the other hand, closed up the Tavern and came dragging in about two thirty in the morning. God, I didn't realize I knew that many songs from the sixties. What an evening! We told everyone good night at the dock and sloshed on to our respective vessels. I could hear snoring coming from the main cabin. Essie turned to me.

"Normally, I rush to get asleep before John does. He sounds just about like an eighteen wheeler going up a steep grade when he gets going. I'll never get to sleep."

It came out of me so naturally that in looking back, I'm still surprised.

"No problem, Essie. My berth is a queen size. Captain's quarters you know. You're invited."

"I accept the Captain's kind offer. I'll be right back. Don't want to sleep in these clothes."

Though I'm in pretty darned good shape for someone as young as I am, I'm still a little apprehensive about my overdeveloped areas. I went ahead and stripped down to my skivvies, dabbed a little extra dry under my arms, and squirted two drops of Old Spice on my neck. No, I always do that before bedtime to keep my sheets smelling fresh. My sheets, oh my Gawd, well, they'll just have to do. I jumped under the covers and adopted my most casual of poses, head on the pillow, right arm under my head. I have to tell you here, I REALY liked what Essie was wearing when she came down the companionway to my cabin. It started at her toes, the nails painted a bright red and adorning the end of two very dainty feet, went up two legs, shaved like a piece of silk, to a wonderfully athletic rear end and narrow waist, continued on to a pair of breasts that looked like they should have been on the body of an eighteen year old. They were full, well rounded and best described as perky little devils. From there up,

161

well, I really don't remember. I always thought her face was spectacular and I had already seen that, so I think that maybe I stopped the inspection when I got to her breasts. She ever so un-affectedly laid down by my side, and did she ever smell better than Old Spice. At that very instant, I reflected for just a second on how special this moment was. Here was a woman that I found beautiful in every way who wanted to share my bed with me. I raised the sheet up so she could slide closer. I buried my head in her dark curly hair and made the conscious decision that I would enjoy exploring every nuance and curve of her body, even if it took a very slow hand a very long time. Her face had the most childlike innocence about it and yet, she was at that moment, the sexiest woman I had ever known. I couldn't resist gently kissing her lips while I cradled her face between my hands. It was the longest of kisses. Well, I don't want to bore you with a bunch of details. That would be kind of like taking an airplane ride to Ta-hiti and trying to describe each individual cloud I saw out of the window of the plane. I'll suffice to say that this was a night of destiny, pre-arranged thousands of years before we were even born. We were supposed to be together. Nothing in my life ever came so naturally or felt so correct. Our passion throughout the night only reinforced that feeling. It had to be almost dawn be-fore we collapsed into a deep sleep; our bodies wound together like line on the spool of tangled fishing reel.

Cappy and Essie

Chapter Nine

The sun seemed to burst into our cabin. We could smell coffee and hear John Silver messing about in the galley. He yelled to us.

"Cappy, I hope that the cook is in there with you. If she ain't, we need to put an add in Latitudes and Attitudes for another one cause she's jumped ship. Had to make the coffee myself this morning, so it's probably a little stronger than you would normally have gotten."

Without hesitation or embarrassment, Essie responded.

"The cook is alive and very well, John Silver. I'll be in there shortly to fix some breakfast."

"Don't get up for me. I know you guys were up most of the night worrying over whether or not I'd be able to get the engine going today. Sounded like you might have even been cleaning some parts for me. Tell you what, I'm going to go up to the marina and have a couple more cups of coffee with Shanny and Stephen, talk boat stuff, you know. Be back in no less than an hour."

"Thanks, John. We owe you."

Essie started rubbing her sweet, soft hands on my chest.

"I love your body. I hope it's in top shape."

"Why is that?"

"Because, you have just been drafted into the NFL of love. Now, let's just check out your equipment. Whoa, it beat you up. Let's try and catch up before it gets away."

Needless to say, we barely took care of the morning duties

in the time John had allotted for us. When he returned, Essie informed him.

"I've decided to not only be the cook, but the Cabin Boy as well. The Captain has duties that need taking care of and have been being neglected by an insensitive crew. I'm rectifying that as of today."

John knew only too well the meaning of all the innuendoes.

"This means, I can have the forward cabin and the V-berth now?"

"Consider it yours, am I correct, Captain?"

"I never argue with the Cabin Boy."

John smiled as he said,

"Good, that's settled. Now what about some chow? We've got an engine to get going."

Two hours later, John and I were back up to our elbows in grease. We methodically reassembled the diesel, installed the new filters and changed the oil. We then, in anticipation that we had done everything properly, wiped the engine down thoroughly to where it looked like new.

"OK, Cappy, keep your fingers crossed and go fire her up."

With great optimism, I hit the glow plug for thirty seconds and then the starter switch. She ground and ground but didn't start. This process continued for another five or so tries. Finally, John did what he said he hated to do; he used the starting fluid. The engine seemed to like that and after a few tries, she turned over and started. Smoke poured out of the exhaust and she sputtered a few times, almost dying as small pockets of air still in the fuel line passed the injectors. Within five minutes, she was purring like a kitten. We were elated. Past his grease covered face, John's white smile shown through massively as he suggested to us.

"This is a day for celebration. The sun is already over the yardarm. I'm ready for a Corona and lunch. Then, an evening downtown were I will attempt to find my own Cabin Boy. But first, I'm heading up to the marina showers where I will try, unaided by props, hidden mirrors or trick photography, to remove all the hot water from their system."

"Sounds good, John. You deserve it. I'm going to straighten up a little more and I'll be right behind you."

Essie and I, both smiling heavily throughout the morning kept finding ways to touch each other as we moved about the cabin. When the urge became too strong, I'd embrace her and lay another kiss on her. I was continually surprised that she not only offered no resistance to my advances, but seemed as anxious to receive my affection as I was to give it.

We both grabbed a towel and started up the dock towards the marina showers. Calypso has a shower on board, but when we're staying at a marina, it's best to use theirs, as we have a hundred-gallon fresh water holding tank and when it's gone, it has to be refilled. Likewise, the toilet facilities empty into a holding tank that must be pumped out when it's full. Far better to share these problems with the marina. At the transient docks where overnighters are tied up, I saw our friends aboard Memories and Forever Young untying their lines. They were apparently shoving off on their way back north. Thank God, I was heading in the other direction with winter bearing down on us. But, they were both active businessmen and could only afford to be gone a few weeks at a time. This Florida trip they were returning from was the longest either of them had done. I was more than quite surprised to see John Silver be the recipient of a friendly embrace and handshake from both Ronnie and Eddy. It was as if they were old friends. If he knew them, it was a shame he didn't come into the Tavern with us the previous evening and share their company. John threw their bow lines to them, waved good-bye and continued towards the showers.

Eddy and Jennifer Parker with Essie

They had cleared the docks as we approached and Essie and I waved to them as they left. They were a neat bunch of people and having friends like them in New Bern made the prospects of eventually having to go back a lot more palatable. As we got to the showers, Essie continued to the women's and I entered the men's where the steam from John Silver's wash-down was as prolific as promised. I began to take off my clothes and fight my way through the steam to the other shower.

"John, I didn't realize you knew the Cousinos and the Youngs. Great folks, huh?"

"Who are they?"

"They were the people you were just with on the dock when they shoved off."

"Just met them this morning, borrowed a wrench from the folks on the Hunter. Yeah, they seemed nice enough."

That just flat out struck me as odd. That was not a 'we just met' hug that they were laying on John Silver and face it, with his scraggily looks, not many complete strangers are going to be volunteering embraces his way. It didn't make sense. I had to ask.

"You just met them today?"

"That's right, they were kind enough to lend me an open end 7/16 box wrench. I took it back to them just as they were leaving. Yeah, they said they were friends of yours. I'd have liked to have been able to spend a little time with them, though. Maybe when we all get back to New Bern."

I had grown to trust John Silver. It was apparent that he had a speckled past, but I had no reason to not trust him. His character seemed to be more deeply rooted than what was on the surface and the person down deeper seemed imminently trustworthy to me. But, something was going on here. My curiosity was peaked. Why would he be concerned about me knowing that he was not a stranger to Ronnie and Eddy? I would be watching carefully for any other chinks in his armor.

Calypso was ready to resume our trip. We were clean, she

was basically straight and we had one more evening to explore the delights of Charleston. Essie wanted to go on a walk through the historical district and look into any of the old homes that were open to the public. After my experience with the old farmhouse, all I saw was work when looking through an antique structure. But, I have to admit a certain fascination with old things. I just would never again try and make something old into something new. John Silver did not share this interest.

"You guys go on without me. I'm going to start looking in earnest to fill that cabin boy vacancy. I'll either be here or somewhere else when you get back."

"That makes sense, John. See you in a few hours."

As Essie and I walked down the old cobblestone streets, she oohed and aaahhhed at practically every old home. For women, looking at beautiful homes is like me looking at boats. At least Essie got equal enjoyment from boats also. We were like two high-school kids still incredulous over our great fortune in finding each other. There were obviously greater forces than ourselves driving us together. We were just passengers on this train, enjoying the ride and excited to see where it was going to end up. Still, I couldn't shake the little incident with John earlier in the day. I explained the event to Essie. She came back with the common sense answer that I had grown to expect from her.

"I judge John Silver by how he treats me, nothing else. I don't care where he came from and what his resume looks like. I'm sure mine would not be very impressive to most people."

"What about the jail thing? Apparently, he's spent time in more than one, and he actually said he'd been in Sing Sing. That's a pretty heavy place from what I understand."

"I'm not saying to just go through life with your head in the sand till your body gets chopped off. I mean, it is a little disconcerting, but he seems to me to be a pretty decent guy, a lot of fun and you have to admit, he's a big help on the boat. Did he promise you any more than that or try to hide the fact he'd been in prison?"

"No, that's a fact. He doesn't act ashamed about it at all. He's always been right up front about it. I agree, I don't think he'd do anything to harm either of us or Calypso, but I'd give two bucks to hear his entire story."

"It'll come out eventually. We'll be having a beer in Key West or Freeport one night in January and he'll just open up and tell us the whole story. Till then, I'm OK with him."

"And I guess I am too. So that's that. Now, let's pick out one of these old mansions. Keep it under a couple million though, I still have plans for a bigger boat."

"Count on it."

It was the middle of October. The sun was setting very early in the day. As it disappeared the temperature dropped right along with it. I put my arm around Essie and walked briskly back to the marina. Calypso was empty and dark. We went below and cut on the small electric cabin heater. I prefer the quick, warm heat from the propane cabin heater, but once again, the marina provided the electricity and we had to keep the propane tanks full ourselves. So, we always saved the propane for when we were anchoring out. Essie went to the galley counter and began washing a few dishes that had been left out earlier in the day. John had been moving his stuff to the forward cabin that Essie had been using before moving aft with me. There was quite a bit of stuff just laying on the bunk and stacked on the shelves either side and above it. There was one envelope laying open on the floor and as I reached down to pick it up, I noticed it was a statement from a prominent New York bank. I know I shouldn't have done it, but resistance was not in me at the moment. I opened it and looked at the ledger. The statement was not John Silver's. It was for a Bob Leisey. I knew that name. This statement was very thick, probably four times what mine usually was. The entries were mostly to corporations or financial institutions. At the top was the balance entry. I practically fell over when I saw the number, which had been circled by hand with a red pen. The end of the month balance was six hundred, forty nine thousand and some odd change! I studied the balance sheet more thoroughly now that my interest had been basically set on fire. There were also a number of entries that had been highlighted with a yellow magic marker. Essie casually looked over at me.

"And you are reading what?"

"Somebody's bank statement."

"John's?"

"Nope, Bob Leisey's."

"The only Bob Leisey I know is the Wall Street investment banker who went to jail for under the table stuff, you know insider trading. He paid a fine of over a billion bucks and still had a fortune left. That's obviously not his."

"Well, if it's not, it's a very rich Bob Leisey just the same. His friggin' checking account has over a half million bucks in it."

"Let me see that."

Essie took the ledger and her eyes followed the same path down it mine had.

"Holly Shit. What do you suppose John is doing with

this?"

"I hate to say it. But I bet, no good."

Essie looked sad as she was coming to the same conclusion.

"But, how in the Hell would he get hold of this?"

"I'm pretty sure I know where he got his hands on it."

"Where?"

"Do you remember when we had the tour of Melinda Katz's yacht?"

"How could I forget your brush with Elvira, queen of darkness?"

"Don't be mean, Essie. You remember the office the Steward closed while we were looking in?"

"That's right, the Leisey Corporation. Oh Jeez, you think John lifted the bank information when he was aboard?"

"It's staring us right in the face. He's been to jail at least twice, once for robbery he told me to my face. It looks to me like the handwriting is pretty damn clear."

"I'm having another horrible thought."
"What's that?"

"Before I accuse him of anything, I need to copy down the number off this account."

I quickly got a pencil from the nav station and jotted down the number. No sooner had I finished writing, than John Silver stepped into the cockpit.

"John Silver, ace first mate and still without a cabin boy, reporting for duty."

I slipped the bank statement back into the envelope and dropped it on the bed where I had to assume he intended it to be. A second later, John was in the salon with us.

"Well, I had a pleasant afternoon. Visited the Tavern. John and Sami were there and said to tell you guys howdy. I told them we'd be outta' here early tomorrow and they said to wish you the best if they didn't see you before you got away. Nice people. I like this town. If it were just a little warmer in the winter and the water was clear, this would be perfect. But, the Keys are calling. Anybody for a nightcap?"

"Sure, I'll take a little coffee with a shot of Bailey's in it. Essie?"

I could see in her face the indecision about how to act around John Silver after the new revelation.

"Yeah, I'd love one."

"Alright young lady, I'll fix it for us. John, what'll you be having?"

"Just a Corona for me, thanks. Don't like to switch horses in the middle of the stream."

I also hoped that my new concerns about John Silver didn't register on my face. I didn't want to ruin our friendship, or upset the cruise, but I also didn't want to be caught with my pants down. If in an effort to keep our trip, (or was it John's escape?) viable and afloat, had he given the account number he stole off the yacht to my credit card company? If that had occurred, when I exceeded my limit I had been an accomplice to stealing. Shit, what should I do? Was this amiable, happy go lucky guy a criminal? Was he dangerous and therefore, were we in danger? I was not going to jump off the deep end, but these things needed to be addressed immediately. I certainly wouldn't do it while Essie was here, just in case he flipped out when I approached him. We spent the next hour making small talk. Essie and I regrouped, composed ourselves and acted naturally. I was glad she had seen the evidence of my concerns so I didn't have to keep all this to myself. About ten PM, I suggested it was time to hit the sack.

"Well, we have to be up and out of here with the outgoing tide early tomorrow, so I guess we better turn in."

I put my arm around Essie and as we started to leave the salon and head outside to the cockpit on our way to our cabin, John queried us.

"Hey guys, has anyone been going through my stuff?"

It was very easy to spot the bank statement envelope in his hand. Only one response came to mind and I figured it would have the most ring of truth to it.

"Oh, there was a couple things laying on the floor at the end of the V-berth there, I just threw them on the bed. Didn't mess anything up did I?"

He looked at the envelope then at me. There was a look in his eyes, a serious deep look that I had not seen in him before.

"No, everything seems to be here. Just concerned that I keep all my stuff together. No problem."

We continued to my cabin.

"See you in the morning, early, John."
"Right on, Cappy."

Essie turned to me as we lay together.

"I feel sure he knew you'd gone through it."

"No, I'm going to try to not be paranoid about this. He

responded just about like I would have expected. He's fine. Let's think about this on the way to Jacksonville. I'll watch out for anything out of the ordinary and you do the same."

"More out of the ordinary than today? I hope not."

"I'm sure everything will be fine. Now, I've got this really sore spot in the middle of my back. I'd rub it myself, but I can't reach it. You don't suppose I could talk you into, well, I hate to beg. But, you know."

"I hate to see a grown man beg like this. OK, OK, shut up. I'll take care of it. Is this the spot?"

"Nope, you just keep rubbing everywhere and I'll tell you when you hit it. Nope, not there, not there, ummhhh, you're getting closer, I can feel a little relief, closer still..."

And so the night went. I could forget most any problem when I was holding Essie. I don't know how I could have lived so many years without this.

Morning came quickly. John was already on deck by the time Essie came to. This would not be a time for lingering. We needed to catch the tide. She gave me a monstrous hug with the promise of more later, threw on her clothes and headed to the galley to get some coffee and a little cereal going. I joined John on deck. He was cheery and seemed one hundred percent as always.

"Morning, Cappy. If you'll fire her up, she can be warming up while you sign out at the office. I'll be down to two dock lines by the time you get back."

I walked up to the marina office. John and Sami were up this morning and had a serious look on their faces. I asked if there was a problem and they got my juices going without even realizing it. Sami answered.

"We're fine. John just hates to get up this early and the Sheriff's Office called to tell him they were headed this way with some sort of a warrant for one of the boaters here. Happens every once in a while. We've got about a dozen or so live-aboards here and occasionally somebody will write a bad check or their ex-wife's lawyer will find out where they are and have them arrested for failure to keep up their alimony payments. Usually, it's nothing very important. Well, it was sure a pleasure meeting you, Essie and John. Please come back and stay with us when you head back up north. We'd love to hear about your trip."

"You can count on it. What do I owe you?"

"Let's see here. I think about ninety bucks should take care of you. Gave you our little discount we save for friends. Come back now."

"We will. See you later."

Shanny and Stephen were waiting at the slip by the time I got back. They wished us well, Shanny gave me a little hug. Though I didn't really have much money, I tipped them ten bucks each. I just liked them, I guess. Maybe I was starting to miss my own kids a little. As I stepped aboard and took the wheel, Stephen threw the dock lines to John on the deck and I revved up the rejuvenated engine and we backed out of the slip. I looked back and waved to the kids several times and the very last time, I could see the brown and white side of a Sheriff's car pulling in. After that, I didn't look back. I figured, if it's critical, they'll come get us. In the back of my mind, I couldn't help but think about the possibility that somehow Essie and I were becoming co-conspirators with John Silver. For the moment, I was willing to give him the benefit of the doubt. But if the authorities showed up asking questions, I was prepared to sing like a parakeet.

Chapter Ten

The Intracoastal Waterway winds through the low-country of South Carolina like a water-moccasin twisting and slithering along a muddy bank. The old myth about this section of the ICW is that you can pass another boat going in the other direction on just the other side of a mud bank and they're actually going in the same direction as you, and a day ahead. You can't make this section any faster by rushing, so we just sat back in the cockpit and enjoyed the scenery. Wild palms were showing up with some regularity now as well as the occasional glimpse of an alligator. They always lend a festive feel to hopping overboard. Though normally very shy and un-aggressive, they have been known to occasionally ingest a swimmer or two. It certainly made me think twice about getting in the water. It would be a fair statement to say that this was a wild section of the ditch. I loved to see old Mother Nature in her natural state and was enjoying the ride. As the sun came up brightly, the late fall air warmed considerably and we were having a very mild day, probably around sixty-five degrees. We shed our coats in an attempt to soak up all the sun possible. Soon, we would be far enough south to pack up our foul weather gear and jackets for the winter. Today was just a sampler of what was to come. Essie had become much more attentive to me and I was enthralled by everything she did. Just watching her move around on deck was fascinating. She was confident and never asked for help to do anything that she could possibly do on her own. Yet, she retained a wonderful femininity about her that set my heart in motion. I was a little afraid of getting involved with a woman and yet excited by the same prospect. John Silver was his same old affable self. He stayed busy doing worthwhile seaman projects, including everything from splicing dead ends on the halyards to washing out the anchor locker. There was no concern of hidden problems on his face and he was every-bit as cheerful as the day we left. It was hard to think of him as a criminal, especially one who might be perpetrating some nefarious scheme while we traveled towards the sun. We had a lunch underway that Essie put together. Eggbeaters, bacon and cheese on an English muffin. She called them muffin-whichs. Wow, were they ever great tasting. The day was uneventful and yet magical in its simplicity. It was what cruising is all about. I realized that I had quit looking at my wristwatch and hadn't thought about Dalton Smythewick for several weeks. I never wanted to forget the feeling I had the day I quit. To this point, it was one of the highlights of my life. I was coming to grips with the possibility that I was never cut out to work a regular job and be a steady paycheck for a family. As despicable as that may seem, I must have been a gypsy from day one. But, come to think of it, who is made to report to some four foot by six foot cubicle and stare at a computer screen eight to ten hours a day? After a few years, your body turns to lard, your mind is fried and you're so damned depressed about it all that you just give up. If you're sitting there right now and that describes you, just go tell your Dalton Smythewick to kiss your ass and run out the door and follow your wildest dreams. That, my sons and daughters is what your short stay on this big planet is all about. I was at peace with my choices. For better or worse, I was where I wanted to be. There was, of course, the nagging realization that I was still married and yet becoming increasingly enamored, or should I say falling in love with Essie, someone born of the same cloth as me. Stop; don't even think about those things yet. There's plenty of time to see what is going to happen. Hell, Essie may not be interested in a long-term relationship with me, or anyone, for that matter. I'm getting ahead of reality here.

At dusk, we found a lovely little cove and pulled in for the night. As the anchor set, it became apparent that a pretty strong current was running through here. John double-checked the CQR anchor to make sure she was set. I put Calypso in reverse and backed down hard on it till I was sure we weren't going to break free during the night and wind up beached or in the path of a tug pushing barges. I'd done that once and didn't need a repeat performance to savor the emotions. We paused for a moment on deck to watch for any movement of Calypso in relation to the dark silhouette of the shoreline. I drew a deep breath as I noticed two large dark shapes slip off the nearest bank and disappear into the muddy water under us. Alligators still made me very nervous.

Now, a captain and more than likely anybody cruising on a boat gets to know the movements and sensations their boat makes at anchor. I had gotten to the point that I could feel any shift or change of motion when at anchor. It therefore, woke me up when the tide shifted around two AM and Calypso began to swing around a hundred eighty degrees on her anchor rode. Essie, lying beside me, arm gently laid across my chest, also awoke.

"Tide starting to go out?" she sleepily asked me.

"I think so. She'll tighten up from the other side in a minute or two. That CQR is a tough anchor to break free."

After about five minutes, the boat didn't appear to be pulling against the anchor. There was the remote possibility that it had lost it's set and we were slowly dragging it through the muddy bottom. I figured it was worth a look.

"I'm going to get up and check it. Won't hurt to know it's OK. We'll sleep better knowing."

Essie sat up.

"I'm going with you. I want to see how full the moon got anyway."

We put on our jackets and went topsides. As I stepped into the cockpit, it was apparent that the wind had picked up considerably. Essie followed behind. I could hear John moving about below. He had apparently been awakened also.

"Cappy, you checking the anchor?"

"Yeah, Essie and I are up, thought it wouldn't hurt. The tide has changed and she swung around, but I don't think she re-set."

"Well, let me know if you need some help."

"I'm sure we can handle it, John. Just roll over."

I went forward to examine where the rode went through the bow chocks. The line was not leading straight off the bow as it should be under load. Instead, it went towards the stern of the boat as if it were snagged. I called to Essie.

"The rode is fouled. Can you see if it's caught on something towards the stern?"

"Headed that way."

In only a second she reported back.

"I see the problem, it caught on the stern cleat as she came about. I'll free it."

"Be careful."

"I will."

Essie leaned out towards the end of the stern where the line was fouled on the far outside cleat. This was on the very outside corner of the stern of the boat. I watched her leaning out and was headed back to make sure she didn't fall over when she said.

"Got it. She's free now. Should catch in just a second and we'll turn."

What Essie didn't see was the slack line lying alongside the deck twisted around her foot and as soon as the line snapped taught, it instantly pulled her feet out from under her. In less than a second she was over the side and into the dark water. She was in the cold, swiftly moving water so fast, she didn't have time to even call out. I was afraid she might have gotten a mouthful of water the moment she hit. As dark as the night and water was, I visualized her slipping under the surface and never coming up. I began to fantasize that I was seeing dark shapes leaving the bank everywhere headed towards where she went in. I was in a state of panic. I yelled for John as I literally jumped to where Essie had gone over.

"John, Essie's overboard!"

John almost beat me there, pulling up his blue jeans and zipping the fly as he arrived.

"The anchor rode caught her foot and pulled her over, Jesus, I can't see her!"

"Cappy, run to the bow and give me slack on the rode the moment I reach her. I'll call you. Don't want to cut her foot off or loose her before I can get to her."

With that, he just dove in, right behind her. In two strokes, he was holding the anchor line and dove down in a line with where it went under the surface. He broke the surface long enough to yell.

"Slack, right now!"

I untied the rode from the forward cleat and threw about

four feet of the slack towards John. The boat started to turn with the current. God, what was I going to do if he didn't surface with her soon? That was a scenario that I would worry about for many years after that night, for John surfaced like a blue whale, holding beautiful Essie with his right arm, a hold on her so tight that an octopus could have done no better. He cried out to me.

"Cleat her back off and extend the boat hook before we get carried past you."

The current was screaming past Calypso as she tightened against the anchor once again. I leapt over the coach roof and grabbed the boat hook, extending it with one twist and a strong pull. As they came alongside, I pushed the end of the hook towards John's outreached hand and held tightly on the other end. He grabbed hold with his free hand. I now had the full weight of John and Essie as he had no free hands to stroke with. I guided them towards the swim ladder off the stern.

"Grab it on the first pass John. I won't be able to hold you against the current."

"Count on it!"

John put a death grip on the ladder. I reached down and grabbed Essie's arm. She was limp in my grip and I gave every ounce of effort I could muster and pulled her aboard with one sweep. I could see John was coming up by himself so, I shouldered Essie and carried her into the cockpit enclosure, John right behind me. She was not breathing on her own and I administered CPR for the first time since my Red Cross training over five years previous. I prayed as I worked on her and was shortly rewarded with a burst of air and water from her mouth followed by a round of the most beautiful coughing and throwing up that one could possibly imagine. She came to and then began to shiver. John produced towels and a dry blanket.

"Let's go below and get some heat on, Cappy. As cold as I am, she must be freezing."

As I looked at John Silver, standing there completely drenched and shaking with cold, I knew that I had just incurred a debt of mammoth proportions. Even if he turned out to be the guy who trained Ted Bundy, I was going to stick with him through whatever problems he had. He helped me get Essie down below into the main salon. We made up the dinette into a double berth across from the galley. We could heat it up quicker there using the propane galley stove. John shut the companionway doors and I began to peel off Essie's shirt and jeans. As her jeans came off, I noticed that a considerable amount of blood was building at the cuff. Where the rope had caught her, just above her ankle, was a deep gash. It didn't take but one look to know she needed stitches and we were hours away from help, even if the Coast Guard would send out a chopper and fly her to a hospital. She just couldn't bleed unabated for that long. She was still pretty much out of it, so I suggested to John that we stitch her up ourselves, right then. He went through the storage compartment under the V-berth till he found my fishing gear and retrieved a small spool of eight-pound monofilament fishing line. I grabbed a container of rubbing alcohol and several wash cloths. We cleaned the cut with the alcohol and determined there were no severed arteries. While John continued pouring alcohol and aligning the sides of the wound for me, I carefully stitched her up, eventually using over a dozen stitches. Thank God, she was still out. With the last stitch, the bleeding became more of just an ooze and I smeared some antibacterial cream all over the surface of the cut. I continued to dry her hair with a towel and John finally went forward and stripped out of his wet clothes. When he returned, he started a pot of hot coffee. Once Essie quit shivering, I helped her to sit up. We thought it made sense to get her awake good and see how her reasoning was before we let her go to any extended sleep. She slowly came around and I got her to try a little of the coffee. She had no clue what had happened, that she had been overboard or basically anything prior to going out to check the anchor. She could hardly believe it when we told her the details.

"You guys saved my life."

As much as I would have liked to just lower my head, shrug my shoulders and say something like, 'gosh missy, twern't nothin', I had to give credit to the real hero.

"It was John you owe your life to. He didn't think one second before he jumped in after you. I was pretty much dumbfounded. It was a damned awesome thing to witness. John, I really owe you, man."

"You guys would have done the same for me. That's what friends are all about, isn't it?"

"If I ever doubted it, I don't now."

John pointed to Essie's leg.

"Cappy did do a fine job of sewing you back together. Looks like a plastic surgeon did it."

"I didn't even know I was cut. Man that's sore. It looks pretty good though, kind of like an over-hooked mackerel."

"Sorry, all I had was fishing line. We soaked it in alcohol before we used it. I believe it's going to be fine."

Essie held out her arms and motioned for us both to give her our heads for squeezing, which we did. I could feel the relief pouring out of my body. I am still amazed at how easy it is to loose someone on a boat, how quickly it can all happen. I determined that for the remainder of the trip, safety concerns were to go up in priority, a lot.

The next morning found a sore but healing Essie. She tried not to show any residual effects, but it was apparent that her ankle hurt and she favored it. We looked closely at it for any signs of infection but found the color to be good and a line of dried blood just under the stitches indicating that it was healing better than we had any right to expect. Of course, I used the sickness angle as an excuse to go over and hug her maybe, twenty or thirty times during the day. By evening, we would be near Hilton Head, South Carolina. We had not intended to put in there, but we all agreed that a little shore time might be good in case Essie's ankle developed any problems. I had always wanted to see the little red and white striped lighthouse there so the prospect of spending a night was just fine with me. I wanted John to know that I was now a staunch ally and that if he had any legal problems following him or was in the midst of a mistake, that I would do anything I could to help him. I felt I should say something to him before we got to the harbor. God only knows what might be waiting there to greet us. About a half-hour out, while we were enjoying the first Corona of the evening, I broached the subject.

"John, I haven't been totally honest with you."

"How's that, Cappy?"

"Remember when you asked if anyone had been going through your stuff?"

"I do."

"Well, I had picked up a bank statement that had fallen on the floor when you moved to the V-berth. I saw that it belonged to someone else. Bob Leisey to be precise. There was a huge balance in it. I know it's not my business, but with your past history,"

"You mean my being in jail, right?"

"That's right. I was just thinking that rather than have you take some huge risk going after some ill-gotten money; I'd rather just lend it to you. I owe you big time. Essie means a tremendous amount to me and you saved her life."

I looked over at her and Essie just smiled. I was very, very close to using the "L" word but forced myself to refrain at just the last second. She just smiled back and listened as I continued.

"So, what I'm saying here, John. We'd rather just have you along and if we have to stop occasionally and work to keep going, that's just fine with us. I think the authorities were right behind us when we left Charleston."

"Well, that may be so, but it's nothing I want to involve you in. You'll be better off not knowing my full history. It's nothing that will get you hurt. It would just complicate your life. I don't think either of you need that right now. If it gets to the point that I need some help, I'll ask for it. Now, I'd really prefer, as much as I think of both of you, that we don't talk about this again. Deal?"

"That's fine with us, John. I just wanted you know that we're here for you. You understand that, don't you?"

He winked at us as he replied.

"I do, and you don't know how much your support means

to me, both of you. Now, I need another Corona. Beautiful sunset, huh?"

I could only think, God, is he cool under pressure. I couldn't see even an iota of concern in him over this revelation. Whatever he was up to, it was not the first time he had ever been involved in something of this nature. This was not foreign soil. We had offered support. He knew where we stood and there was really nothing more we could do unless he asked for our help. I still hoped deep inside that this would not end up with all of us going to prison. If I was going to be bunking down with somebody for years, I wanted it to be Essie, not Big Daddy Wilson or Vinny the Fist.

The rotating light from Hilton Head began to radiate on the horizon. It was just about sundown. I really was getting excited about visiting this quaint harbor town. I didn't realize just how exciting it was going to be. Just as the lights of the buildings surrounding the harbor began to grow larger, a boat approached us head on. It was running at speed, with a spotlight on the bow. As they approached, they slowed and the large orange stripe on the white hull quickly gave away their identity. It was another Coast Guard cutter, identical to the one that escorted us in at Charleston. However, this did not appear to be a visit we were looking forward to. From the bridge of the cutter, a crewmember with an electronic hailer asked us to go to channel sixteen on the VHF, which I did, heart pounding in my throat.

"Go ahead, Coast Guard. This is Calypso."

"Switch to channel twenty two alpha, Calypso."
"Roger, switching to twenty two."

"Calypso, this is the US Coast Guard. Sir, we respectfully request you bring your vessel to a complete halt here and allow us to board."

"Not a problem, Coast Guard. But what is the nature of this boarding? Is there some problem?"

"We'll discuss that on board if you don't mind, Captain."

The cutter pulled alongside and two crewmembers boarded us. I walked up to meet them. Essie and John remained in the cockpit, Essie nervous beyond all reason and John, still calmly sipping on his second Corona. The older Coastie, with more brass on his uniform approached me.

"Skipper, how many people do you have on board your vessel?"

"Three total, myself and two crew. A woman and a man."

"Do you have identification of all your crew on board?"

"Well, I certainly do and I would imagine my crew both do as well."

"Could we examine your identification, please?"

"Of course. I'll go below and get my wallet."

"We'll wait here, skipper."

As I passed through the cockpit I related to John and Essie what they wanted. Essie said,

"I'll get my driver's license."

John said nothing.

"What about you, John, got your driver's license with you?"

"Nope, nothing requires me to carry it with me. We're not traveling out of the country and I was afraid I might lose it overboard. Tell 'em I can get it in a couple days, if it's worth subpoenaing me over."

"Boy, that's probably not going to be received real well."

"I'll talk with 'em." Give me your licenses and you stay here."

I was only too willing to let John handle this. He seemed very calm and rationale. I was hoping this was not going to result in some sort of shootout. John walked forward while we remained in the cockpit. I could see him hand the IDs to the senior officer. They were in a deep discussion for about ten minutes. They returned to the cutter and we could hardly restrain ourselves when John stepped back in the cockpit.

"What was that all about, John?"

"Nothing serious, mostly a case of mistaken identity. However, just to be cooperative, they want you to follow them into the harbor, which I told them you would do. Tie up on the long pier directly in front of the lighthouse and I'm going to go visit with them for a while. Nothing big, trust me."

God, I wanted to trust him. I was beginning to feel like the parole board at a prison listening to a convicted axe murderer explain that he was totally rehabilitated and truly sorry for the eighteen or so people he had beheaded. I just didn't know what to believe. The Coast Guard motored slowly ahead of us and pulled to the far end of the long pier John had mentioned. They shined a spot behind them indicating where they wanted me to tie up. Two Coasties waited on the dock for us to throw them our lines. They quickly secured us. John came up from below with a jacket on and a small leather valise under his arm. He directed us to just stay calm, go ashore and enjoy the evening and he'd be back shortly. The Senior Officer was waiting on the dock for John. They didn't cuff him or act harshly with him in any manner I could detect. They walked off together to a dark blue sedan with gold letters on the door indicating it was a Coast Guard vehicle. John hopped in with the officer and they sped off. I looked at Essie.

"What in the hell do you think this is all about?"

She was just as bewildered as I was.

"All I can say is, I don't think the US Coast Guard gets involved in things like past due alimony, or bounced checks. I don't feel real good about this. It would be nice if John thought enough of us to confide in us about what was happening here."

"Well, let's get cleaned up and do just what John suggested. We can get a burger and just wait for his return."

We found a small cafe close by and though quite nervous, I managed to inhale a couple beers and Essie polished off a half bottle of White Zinfandel. I could tell her ankle was bothering her some. Perhaps we should get it looked at tomorrow, even if it meant the prison infirmary. But, I did trust John when he said we were in no trouble and not to worry. I didn't have any good reason, but I just trusted him. This guy did save Essie and I promised him my support. In only a couple of hours, the evening would really begin to get interesting.

The small cafe we were in served as much as a bar as it did a grill. It seems whenever there is a harbor with sailboats in it that is always the case. I remember the words a Scottish friend of mine, Martin Barrie once said. He had just been sailing with us a couple of times and met the sailing crowd. He observed,

"sailing is done ten percent under sail, twenty percent under power and seventy percent under the influence."

I might add that today, Martin and his main squeeze, Darlene are part of our group and keep their own Bristol little sloop in New Bern, with the ice-box normally well stocked with his favorite beverage of choice.

Anyway, from the window of the cafe, I saw a skyline of lights slowly moving into the harbor, a familiar skyline. I didn't even want to have to mention it to Essie, I knew only too well what she thought of the illustrious Miss Katz and I also understood that I was going to have to sever our relationship, or at least modify it considerably the next time we met. I knew this would be hard on Melinda. You don't find men like me on every street corner. It was apparent that the interest shown in me recently by two lovely women was distorting any semblance of a realistic self-evaluation of my charms. I didn't have to point out the yacht to Essie. Very little ever got by her.

"I see that the tramp steamer is pulling into port. I use the word steamer liberally."

"Essie, you have no concerns there at all. Miss Katz is now an old shadow on the wall. She plays no part in my new and improved existence, thanks to my present company."

"Don't tell me, tell her. I'm sure she'll be sending either a limo or a helicopter by shortly to retrieve her boy toy."

"It won't happen, wouldn't happen even if she tried. Listen, I'm far more concerned about John right now. Where do you suppose they could have taken him? It's been several hours."

"I don't know. Where's the closest prison?"

"Don't even think like that. I'm really concerned."

"Well, ask him yourself. Here he comes."

Turning towards the door, I saw a smiling John Silver walking our way. Not a care in the world on his face.

"Sorry I was gone so long. You know, I can take one look around a harbor and pick out where to find you guys every time. Just look for a palm tree near the door and a little neon in the window. Doesn't hurt if they have patio speakers going either, with a Buffett song playing."

"Where in the Devil have you been? We thought you were in jail."

"They don't send people to prison unless they commit some sort of crime, generally speaking. And I'm as clean as the new fallin' snow, as the saying goes."

He motioned for the waitress.

"Hey, can I get a Corona over here?"

"So, what's the deal?"

"I told you, a case of mistaken identity. I just proved I wasn't who they thought I was and they brought me back. Case closed. Damn this beer tastes good. Didn't have any at the police station."

"I would imagine not."

"OK, if you don't want to talk with us about it, that's fine with us. Right, Essie?"

"I suppose so. But they better not come and haul us off to jail, I can assure you of that."

"Not to worry, you guys. I swear, you are a couple of nervous nellies."

Essie volunteered a suggestion.

"OK, let's change the subject then. John, guess what gaudy yacht just pulled into the harbor?"

"Well, let's see. How about the Pussy's Purr or whatever

that battleship was called."

"You guessed it. I swear she's following us."

John smiled as he offered.

"Is old Cappy here that good in the berth? You know, he looks just like a regular guy."

The humor in the situation was beginning to wear thin to me.

"OK, enough you guys. Melinda Katz has no real interest in me and I assure you we've seen the last of her. Remember, she didn't even come over for dinner in Wilmington."

It was about this time that a familiar voice spoke up just behind my head.

"Captain Les, it's me, Carlo. How have you all been? It's very, very good to see you. There was a Dennis Hopper movie on last night. He played this really screwed up psycho."

"Carlo, I'm…we're surprised to see you. What do you do, just drive down the coast following Miss Katz's boat?"

"Oh, no Sir, Captain Les. The back of the boat just opens up and we drive it onto the boat."

"I shouldn't have asked."

Essie said with a touch of cynicism,

"Les, what's the chance we might keep a bicycle on board? I could drive you around when we get to port. You know, get one with a set of wide handlebars for you to sit on."

"I'll take it under advisement."

"So, Carlo, how did you know we were here?"

"You're not very hard to find. I just look for a bar with palm trees out front, or some neon signs in the window, or…."

"OK, Ok, I get the picture. So, what's up?"

He handed me an envelope, once again bearing the gold emblem of the Katz Meow.

"This is for all of you. You'll be coming to our party to-morrow. It's a very special event, I'm told. Everyone on board is extremely excited, though no one has told me why just yet. That usually happens when there is a very special guest coming."

I looked over at Essie.

"Carlo, I appreciate this a lot but I'm afraid you'll have to just tell Miss Katz that..."

Essie took the envelope and stopped me mid sentence.

"We'll be there, Carlo. Thank you so much for tracking us down to invite us."

"It truly isn't hard, I just heard the music outside and....."

"OK, Carlo, OK. See you tomorrow."

Carlo didn't leave as would have been his etiquette with anyone else in the world I'm certain. Hat under his arm, he looked at us and asked,

"Captain Les, how about I join you guys for just one beer?"

We all laughed.

"Sit down, Carlo. You're always welcome at our table."

"Thank you, Captain Les, I really missed you guys."

The evening was splendid, though there was an underlying feeling of things yet to happen relative to John Silver. No doubt, we hadn't come close to finding out the real story of what was going on with him. We found our way back to Calypso, unaided by being sober. Normally, I'm a three beer and out guy, but I guess all of the occurrences of the last two days had pent up a lot of stress in all of us that needed undoing. We all drank a little too much and had a late, fun evening. As we approached the dock, we paid very little attention to a grouping of news vans with satellite dishes on top, set up in the parking lot. Essie crashed immediately, her ankle was better, but still a little sore. John Silver and I sat up in the cockpit philosophizing for another hour. John always struck me as bright, but there were certain times when he came across as a lot smarter than that. Tonight, he seemed to be in a very reflective somber mood I hadn't seen in him before. He studied his words as he spoke.

"Les, I can't tell you how much I appreciate you're having me along on this trip. It has meant a tremendous amount to me."

"Well, it's certainly not over by a long shot."

"I'm afraid it is, at least for me. This will be my last night on board Calypso."

"Why is that? Are the authorities coming for you or something?"

"Nope, but my life is far more complicated than most folks. I've made some big mistakes and have paid dearly for them. Continue to pay in a lot of ways. I needed this trip with you and Essie to try and keep my sanity. I've been running away from things just as much as you have. And tomorrow, I won't be able to run anymore. My little escapade into this simple life onboard Calypso will have to end."

"You're not, well, not going back to prison, are you?"

"In some ways, I am. But not a prison with actual bars. Well, that's enough about me. I will be in touch with you and Essie though, and you'll never be far out of my thoughts. You gonna' marry Essie?"

"Well, I feel like I want to, but actually, I'm not even legally separated yet. I guess I need to go ahead and do that so if Essie does want us to get married down the road, I'd be free to do it."

"Trust me, keep the law on your side. Do it the right way. Well, Captain Les, this has truly been a wonderful time for me. I guess I better turn in. Tomorrow promises to be a quite trying day."

"Anything I can help you with?"

"You've already done more than you'll ever know. Goodnight."

"Night."

Chapter Eleven

I woke up with a slight bit of a headache. Essie had her arm once again, gently stretched out over my chest. That seemed to be her security blanket position and to tell the truth, I had grown very fond it myself. I got up as quietly as possible to try not to wake her. This was to no avail as the moment I cleared the bed, she inquired,

"You getting up, Baby?"

"Yeah, I need to visit the head and then fix up mine. You need some aspirin too?"

"A couple wouldn't hurt. When did you and John get to bed?"

"Very late. We had a nice talk. I really like the guy. I wish I knew the whole story on him. He just doesn't seem like the kind of person that could hurt anybody or do anything worth winding up in prison over."

"I know what you mean. Is he up yet?"

"Don't know. I'll be back in a minute with your aspirin."

I crossed over the cockpit and went to the main salon. I looked into the forward cabin but not only was John no where to be found, but all his belongings were gone. I stuck my head above deck and looked over the marina. He might have gone to the marina showers as he liked an abundance of hot water, but I seriously doubted that was the case. I relieved myself, took three aspirin and put on a pot of coffee. I took a glass of water and several aspirin to Essie.

"John's not up?"

"Up and gone. May be in the showers."

"Oh, so what's on the schedule for today?"

"First, some of my famous homemade blueberry pancakes which I'll make while you slowly get your head together. Then, how about we stroll around Hilton Head and see what the place has to offer?"

"You know me, second gypsy first class."

"OK, pancakes and coffee coming up."

"I didn't mention to Essie that John said he would be leaving today. I'd tell her later, over breakfast after her head quit aching."

While we were eating, I finally broached the subject.

"Essie, I don't think we'll be seeing John anytime soon. He told me last night to tell you how much sailing with us meant to him and that he thought you were the best. He said that last night would be his last night on board."

"Did he say why?"

"Nope, just as mysterious as ever. He did say that he wasn't going back to prison. He just had a bunch of things in his life that required attention."

"I wonder why he didn't wait to tell me good-bye, I mean, for crying out loud, he saved my life."

"I know Baby. Maybe we'll see him before he leaves."

"I hope so, I really liked John."

"I know, Essie. I did too."

John didn't come back to Calypso that morning. We took a rather quiet, somber walk around Hilton Head and were really impressed with what a neat little place it was. As we came back to the marina, it would have been impossible to not notice that the news vans had multiplied considerably, with the main concentration being in the vicinity of Katz Meow. As we got nearer, it became apparent just how large the contingent of news-people actually was. There were probably a dozen or so news trucks, four city police cars working traffic and the crowd, another fifty or so people milling about on foot. All were apparently interested in what was going on aboard the yacht. By now, our curiosity was peaked considerably also. We approached one of the newsmen.

"Excuse me sir, can you tell us what is going on here?"

"There's a social event onboard this yacht tonight and a LOT of celebrities are going to be present. We're all just hoping to get a few shots and maybe a couple of words from the guests."

"For example, who is coming?"

"We're not supposed to share this information." This was, of course, said with a little attitude to let us know our place.

"You can see it tonight on the local news, I'm sure."

"I imagine we'll see it a lot sooner than that since we have an invitation to the party."

Make a note, watch dramatic attitude change with that piece of news.

"You are? Well who are you folks?"

I wouldn't miss an opportunity like this for the world. After all, there were many other large yachts in the harbor.

"We're here on our yacht. Miss Katz always invites us to her parties."

"Miss Katz? I thought Mr. Leisey was hosting this."

"Not so, this is her boat and the invitation was from her."

Essie and I both had the same horrible thought at the same

second. I could see it wash across her face as it tromped across mine. We looked at each other, then left the reporter still asking questions while we walked off.

"Oh my God. The Leisey Corporation. John is going to hit the place tonight. That's what he was after all along. He was trailing the yacht for just the right moment and tonight is it. We've got to intercept him, get to the yacht first and stop him from doing this. We owe him that much."

"OK, Les. Let's come up with some kind of plan. This thing is supposed to start at seven PM and it's four thirty right now. I've got to find something to wear that doesn't look like it's out of the Frontier Woman clothing manual."

We both did our best to try and come up with something half-decent to wear to a major soiree. The best I could do was the one dress shirt I wore to work on the last day and a pair of freshly washed blue jeans. A very casual look. Essie, went back to the tropical summer party dress she wore, for lack of a single dress other than that. But, when she used a little lipstick, combed back her hair and threw on a pair of large gold earrings, she could stop a train. Every time I saw her maxed out like this, I had to wonder what she ever saw in me. I just kept telling myself, don't question fate. Accept the good things as well as the bad. We knew we were going to be early, but the sun was already down entirely by six PM. We made our way through the news crews and reporters, which had doubled again. I really didn't understand why all the fuss. Who the Hell was coming to this thing? The President? We showed our invitation to the police officer at the gangplank and our former tour guide, the steward, showed us the way. We went to the second level above the deck, an area we hadn't seen previously. There was a huge main salon there, maybe twenty feet wide by sixty feet long, which emptied to an outside deck that was awash with party lights. Gentle jazz sounds came from internal and external speakers. A fair description of the massive salon would be an elaborate hotel ballroom. There were any number of crystal chandeliers, polished hardwood floors dotted with Persian rugs, a number of oil paintings that I'm sure weren't picked up at roadside stands, and even a grand piano. A small orchestra was getting ready to crank up and the presence of electric guitars in racks indicated that at some point during the evening, elevator music from the orchestra would be replaced with something a little easier to dance to. Party decorations were everywhere with streamers and even a disco ball hanging from the ceiling. This would be a new experience for me. The grandest parties I'd ever been to where probably thrown by the PTA. If I weren't so preoccupied with keeping an eye out for John Silver, this could be fun. I was also more than a little concerned about how Melinda would be around me. Essie was there and she already had a strong disdain for all things Katz. We were among the first to arrive. I positioned myself in the salon where I had a view of the interior, the outside deck and the gangplank. If John Silver made it on board, I would most likely see him.

Even above the music, the unmistakable sound of a helicopter hovering outside drew my attention. I stepped out onto the deck and surveyed the wild scene in the parking lot. There was definitely a chopper setting down. The police were screening off the area to keep anyone from losing their head over a news item. Lights from the television crews had the area looking like a football stadium getting ready for a night game. There was also a circle of limos starting to build and a crowd starting to move towards the yacht. I strained to see who stepped out of the chopper.

As the passenger disembarked, so many flashbulbs went off and reporters crowding the scene that I couldn't get even a glimpse of who it might be. Well, they were all headed this way. I'd just remain low key, try to look like another painting on the wall and have a visual feast. There was still no sign of John and I was hoping my guess as to what he was up to was wrong.

"Well, good evening Captain Les. Don't you look smashing tonight."

That was a voice I couldn't help but recognize. Melinda Katz came over, splendid in her silk and diamonds. She gave me a buzz on the cheek.

"Melinda, thank you for inviting us to such a spectacular party. This will certainly be an evening for the scrapbook. You know, we met Dennis Hopper when Carlo drove us to Wilmington for lunch. I never did get to thank you for that. He was a really great guy."

"Oh, Dennis, yes I love him. He'll be here tonight. Along with a few other faces I'm sure you'll recognize."

Essie came alongside.

"Oh, and this beautiful creature must be Essie whom I've heard so many nice things about. I am absolutely thrilled to know that Captain Les has such a lovely woman taking care of him. Come here darling, let me get you a champagne and show you off a little."

Essie was taken completely aback by Melinda's friendly overtures and followed her towards a group getting their first drink from one of the many tuxedo sporting waiters. I continued to scan the room. It was about this time that a large murmur arose from the guests as through the doors leading aft came a group of faces anyone in the country would recognize. But, the one that jumped out at me immediately was Jim Grimshaw's. One of my favorite character actors of all time and a face I'd seen for over twenty years in such movies as, THE PEOPLE VERSUS LARRY FLYNT, REMEMBER THE TITANS, THE JACKAL, NORTH AND SOUTH, and countless others. A retired Green Beret officer, he was a war hero long before he started showing up on the silver screen. He strode magnificently across the room, smiling at everyone he passed and not leaving one woman under forty without a kiss. He made his way over to Melinda and Essie.

Photo by David C. Eanes

Cappy with Jim Grimshaw aboard Katz Meow

When he bent over and planted a big one on Essie, she literally dropped her champagne glass. The high toned pitch it made when it shattered indicated that the crystal was of the highest order. Melinda then moved over to Grimshaw's side and latched onto his arm with a death grip that I would imagine he would have trouble getting free of for the remainder of the evening. Throughout the next hour, a parade of who's who's, notables and wannabes with enough connections to get invited flooded Katz Meow. After a round of finger foods, which even included caviar, that I had no taste for, the orchestra was replaced by a more contemporary group. They might have been famous for all I know. I recognized a few of the songs and they sounded exactly like the records. But, they didn't do Buffett, so they couldn't be on my favorite band list. In this mob, finding John would be no easy task. I did have the advantage that in this crowd, he would look like a cactus on a putting green. But still, no sign of him.

Within an hour of our arrival, the crowd had swelled to capacity. There must have been a hundred people on board. The drinks had been flowing like Niagara Falls and I was even beginning to feel the music better. Essie was still wondering around with Melinda, the woman she thought she hated and Jim Grimshaw. He moved from group to group, working the crowd as only a pro could do. I wondered how many hotel room keys he would wind up with before the night was over. I had more than one woman come up to me and ask who I was with and if I wanted to shake a leg. At first I wouldn't because of Essie being there and also because, well, initially, I was sober. Both of those reasons were losing their grip on my conscious mind and finally, there I was, doing the shag with some woman from France wearing what appeared to be see through toilet paper and a lot of makeup. She did smell wonderfully and didn't object to the fact that my dancing was something similar to trying to park a thirty-seven Packard in a sub compact spot. Finally, Essie returned and tapped her on the shoulder.

"You know, I kinda like Melinda. She's not at all what I thought. I think she's just lonely, having all this money and not knowing who her real friends are. We're going to go shopping together tomorrow."

This is just great, I thought. Now they're best friends. Sometimes women are very difficult to understand, at least for me. It was about this time that the crowd was entertained beyond all expectations as Melinda and Grimshaw jumped up on the Grand Piano and proceeded to do a compact version of the Charleston, without so much as a missed step or a near fall. The crowd went wild. It ended with the pair jumping off the piano hand in hand to the floor. We had everything except Lawrence Welk saying,

"tank you, Bobby and uh Sissy!"

I joined the crowd in offering a thunderous round of applause. Essie brought me back to reality.

"Any sign of John? she asked."

"None, maybe I was all wrong. I'm sure we'd have noticed if he were here."

Essie again rattled my cage a little with,

"You don't suppose he could be on board, maybe in the owner's quarters, taking stuff right now, do you? I mean, everyone is up here, why would he show himself? Wouldn't that be kind of stupid? Who would notice? Couldn't we just step outside for some fresh air and sort of look around, inconspicuous like?"

"That's probably a good idea. My head is swimming from all this champagne anyway. I should have stuck with Coronas."

"Me too, but it's so good."

I grabbed Essie's arm and we walked through the room. As we passed Grimshaw, he walked over, kissed her on the cheek and reminded her that she had promised him a dance.

"He's something else, isn't he?"

I have to admit a tinge of jealousy at this point.

"I heard he snores like a racehorse and can't keep a woman. I mean, he's been married like five times."

"Really? You're kidding aren't you?"

"Well, I'm just telling you what I've heard. But, he did fight for his country, so I'm willing to be friendly to him. It'll be fine if you want to dance with him."

"I don't need permission."

"I know, I'm just saying that more than a couple of dances and I start to feel the competition."

She pulled my arm close up to her side.

"Baby, you ain't got nothin' to worry about with me. Besides, he told me that he's dating Demi Moore now. I don't want to ruin things for her, she's had a hard enough life recently, what with breaking up with Bruce and all."

"So, it's Bruce now, not Mr. Willis?"

"Can you feel it? I just seem to fit in with this group."

"I stuck my finger in her ribs and elicited the uncontrolled laughter I knew that would come forth. Ticklish was an understatement.

"OK, OK, I'll be good, Mr. Willis, Mr. Besides, you're far hotter. That better?"

That felt and sounded like just what I wanted to hear.

Chapter Twelve

We walked around the decks, enjoying the surreal scene. As we approached the door to the elaborate office we had noticed before, there was a group of people inside, having what appeared to be a more serious and intimate gathering. We moved closer and leaned against the polished rail, where we had a good line of sight and yet would appear to be just two more guests enjoying the night air.

There were about a dozen or so guests in the more intimate ship's office. They were more or less congregated around a very stylish couple who exuded an air that could only be described as regal. She was tall, dark haired, and pretty much dripping with diamonds. He was polished, short cropped gray hair, black tux, too many teeth and his smallest hand gesture seemed to hypnotize the group around him that were hanging on his every word. Together they were a very important looking couple. He seemed to be pointing to a chart sitting on a tripod in the front of the room under the Leisey Corporation sign. This must be the guy whose money John Silver had a taste for. This guy was, he was, HE WAS JOHN SILVER!!

"Essie, are you seeing what I'm seeing?"

"Shit! That's John! He doesn't even look the same. His hair is cut, and combed. He's clean shaven and even his body language is different. Look how he moves. All his gestures are different. You were right. He is good at whatever he's trying to do here. Maybe he's like a jewel thief, you know, the polished bandit sort of criminal. You saw Steve McQeen in THE THOMAS CROWN AFFAIR?"

"Exactly. What the Hell should we do? We can't just go crashing in there and let everybody know he's a thief."

"I say, we just stay close, go where he goes and see what happens. Worst comes to worse, we can throw him overboard and he can swim to the dock and make good an escape."

"You've had too much champagne, all right."

"Not too good an idea, huh?"

"No."

"OK, we'll just play it by ear."

John worked the group like a maestro. His every move was a study in confidence and practice. It was hard to believe this was our John Silver, but there he was. We could hear the crowd getting louder and louder in the main ballroom. The champagne was working wonders on them. The music was becoming more and more like a top forty radio station play-list. After an hour of our clandestine snooping, Essie and I were getting quite cold. It was about this time that John's group began to file out of the cabin and walk en masse towards the ballroom. We turned our backs to them as they passed. After they had about a twenty-foot lead, we followed, still playing the intimate couple, trying to be alone in a crowd. As John and his entourage entered the ballroom, an amazing thing happened. A loud round of applause came from the large crowd and the band quit playing. We eased in behind them and stood off to the side of the room. We were just out of John's line of sight. While shaking hands with the men and kissing the women as he passed, John made his way towards the front of the room where a small podium stood. It reminded me of the President walking through the crowd to give a State of the Nation address. The group quieted and John cleared his throat, taking a drink from a glass of water as the crowd grew still. He began to speak to the entire room.

"Ladies and gentlemen, friends and associates, on behalf of myself, my beautiful wife, Deborah, and all the employees world wide of the Robert Leisey Corporation, I want to thank you for coming tonight. As you know, the purpose of this wonderful gathering that Deborah has organized for all of us, is to raise money for the Leisey Charitable Trust. All of you, by your presence here, have helped to make this coming year a better one for many poor families. For that, I would like to say once again, thank you. Now, we have some really wonderful wine, great entertainment and no clock telling us when it's time to leave. So, stay as late as you want and if you have a little too much bubbly, we'll get you home. Also, a special thanks to a number of our friends from Hollywood who have come to lend their faces to this charitable endeavor. Don't be afraid to walk up and introduce yourselves. But ladies, be especially careful around Grimshaw, he's single again. Have a wonderful evening."

I looked at Essie.

"Does this mean what I think it does?"

"He's either Robert Leisey, one of the wealthiest men in the country or, he's the greatest thief in history."

"What the Hell was he doing with us for the past two weeks?"

"At this point, I'm lost. Why don't we just let him answer these questions?"

"That's the best idea yet."

We made our way towards the podium where John was shaking hands and receiving a large number of guests. We just took our place in the line and grabbed another champagne each from the steward as he passed. It was very good stuff. As our turn approached to greet this giant of American business, I looked closely at him and could hardly believe the change in his countenance and appearance. Which person was real, John or Robert? He gave us a very broad smile as we came to the head of the line.

"Captain Les, Essie, I am thrilled that you came tonight. I was afraid that the interest my sister had shown in you might have caused Essie to stay away and keep you both from coming. What do you think of our little party?"

"John, as I'm sure you must be aware, this is all pretty mind-boggling to us. What the Hell has been going on? What were you doing with us the past couple of weeks? Melinda is your sister? Jeez, how could you listen to all the gory details and not let on?"

"The ability to say nothing is sometimes a very good tool in my world. Look, let me speak to a few more people and then we can go to my cabin and talk awhile, how's that?"

"We're not going anywhere."

"That's great. Just give me ten minutes."

We watched John, or Robert, work the room for a little while longer. He knew everyone there by name and made it a point to speak to them all. As promised, after about ten minutes, he came back to us and asked us to follow him. We made our way to a private door at the end of the ballroom and upon entering, found a polished brass, circular stairway leading to the next floor. It had a sign reading "Private Quarters" above the first step and its sheer opulence promised that even more extravagance was ahead. It was a promise shortly fulfilled. Now, I've already described the opulence of Katz Meow many times, so let's just suffice to say that the private quarters exceeded anything we had already seen by two or three times.

John walked over to a section of the cavernous owner's stateroom and showed us to a couple of Louis XIV armchairs. Essie and I sat while he brought us each a Corona.

"Here guys, the champagne is good, but nothing beats a cold beer. I'm sorry to have shocked you this way. I really didn't know of a good way to end our time together without you just thinking I was a little well, bonkers. So, I invited you here and exposed you to my world just as you did yours to me for the past several weeks. I have to tell you, I enjoyed yours far more than mine."

"You're kidding John, I mean Bob. You've got everything anybody could even think of."

"That's not necessarily so, Les. I don't have the freedom that anonymity brings with it. Everywhere I go, all day, every day, people with cameras are waiting. I have to be careful about who I associate with, where I go, what I do. In many ways, it's the proverbial case of the bird in the gilded cage."

Essie offered,

"I think you'd probably have trouble getting any sympathy from most people. You're where everyone else is trying to get."

"Then, you should be flattered that you are a step beyond there. You have stepped out of your constraints, freed yourself of your bonds and taken off to find your dreams. You are to be admired and envied."

"Well, we aren't necessarily free of worldly concerns. Sure, we have this minute but we don't know how we will pay for tomorrow."

"No one, is without worldly concerns. That, my friends is not possible under any situation. There is always the need for food, water, shelter, protection from bad elements and even the fury of Mother Nature. God, I'll never forget coming into Charleston in that nor'easter. That's the most alive I've felt in twenty-five years. You can believe me when I tell you that money is not actually up there with any of those things. A wealthy man without food, water, clothing, shelter or most important, friends, has nothing. It's just a part of our worldly concerns. You have taken the step that most people are just flat out afraid to take. You have both said,

"we're tired of the system, we will make our own way in the world, live every minute in pursuit of our dreams."

"That, my friends is what success is all about. And, the willingness to take that risk can often-times overcome the things you saw as obstacles to taking the first step. You just have to believe that things will work out. I am a firm believer that everything always works out, exactly as it's intended to, maybe not the way we foresaw them or not even on our timetable, but they do work out as they are supposed to. Listen, for the past ten years, I've done exactly what I've done with you this past couple of weeks. I let my family and associates know that I'm dropping off the planet for a while and then I just go out to find the real world. I am thrilled that I was able to go along with you aboard

Calypso while you did the same thing. Now, you guys will continue on and I'll be back in a grind that most people could not begin to imagine. I have thousands of people whose jobs and lives depend on what I do, even what I say about things, like the stock market, for example. It's a lot of responsibility and it doesn't go away because I'm tired or just need to be left alone. Don't get me wrong, I'm not looking for sympathy, I'm pretty much happy with my lot, but it is a very busy existence that doesn't lend itself to just leaving. So, what I'm telling you is, I was doing just what you and Essie are doing, running away if only for a short while."

"So, what do you think of my little speech, buying any of it?"

"First, John or Bob, which is it?"

"Come on, Cappy, nobody is really called John Silver. Call me Bob."

"OK, Bob. I see where you're coming from. I do think it might have been better, though, if you had just been straight with us from day one."

"You mean, approach you with a line like, Mr. Pendleton...Hi, I'm Bob Leisey, your friendly billionaire who would just like to hitch a ride on your boat for a few weeks and just pretend I'm somebody else. You'd have bought that?"

"I guess not."

"I actually never lied to you about anything, other than my name, and I chose that one because I always loved Treasure Island, what a story."

"You have sailed a lot haven't you?"

"Oh yeah, I still have a nice boat."

"You do, what kind is it? A power yacht like this?"

"Never happen, its a hundred seventy...."

"Stop, don't even tell me."

"OK, OK, I know where you're coming from. But, if you ever want to take a trip on her, she's all yours, crew included. So, what's your plan from here on out?"

"I suppose that Essie and I will just keep heading South. The Keys, then the Bahamas, just like we talked about."

"That's great, guys. Listen, either Katz Meow or my boat, StarChaser will be in the Caribbean this winter, maybe we can spend a few more days together. Would that be alright? Am I forgiven for my little charade?"

"Hey, that's fine with me. How about you, Essie?"

"I'm with Les, whatever my Captain wants."

"Is she special, or what?"

"You're a lucky man, Les. What do you say we head back to the party? I've got a really special event about to happen out there that I sorta' planned in your honor, Les, kind of a thank you."

"You're kidding?"

"Nope. And listen, I want you both to know that I'm behind your attempt to break free from it all one hundred percent. Or shall I say, twenty-five thousand?"

"You're kidding?"

"Nope, I'm going to leave that limit on your credit card. Just don't go wild and you should be able to travel for a long, long time. I will of course, drop in once in a while to sort of check on my investment, if that's alright with you guys."

"Your berth will always be there for you, John Silver."

Deborah and Bob Leisey, aka "John Silver"

Essie got up and ran over to John and hugged the pure life out of him. I think he was greatly moved. We went back to the party. Essie danced with Grimshaw and Dennis Hopper, hobnobbed with the rich and famous for the evening and then we both, arm in arm, made our way back to our own little ship, in some ways, a finer vessel than even Katz Meow. The next day, Essie did go shopping with Melinda. In the years to come, they would call and visit each other often. I always hoped they didn't do any comparative analysis regarding me. One other thing I really wanted to tell you, but I promised not to actually use his real name, he apparently doesn't play private parties. The special entertainment that John had arranged played till the middle of the night. We had a few beers together and even swapped a couple of sailing stories. And, I knew every word to every song he sang.

So much had happened over the last couple of days that we hated to leave Hilton Head. But, John, or Bob had another life to live and Essie and I still had a dream to follow. We were going to start motoring down the ICW and try to make Jacksonville, Florida in three days. A little peace and quiet time with Essie was beginning to seem like a very nice prospect. Yeah, just the two of us, more palm trees appearing every day, and, if we decided that it was warm enough to do a little nude sunbathing as we poked along, well, there was just the two of us. I started the diesel and Essie took the wheel as I began untying the dock lines. It all seemed a little too quiet when compared with recent events.

I was just about to throw the last dock line ashore when I heard the now familiar sounds of a chopper approaching the marina parking lot. The local police car pulled in the lot and backed off the few people in the area. Within a moment, the chopper began to settle about fifty yards from Calypso. Somehow, I knew that whoever was on the helicopter was headed our way. The departure had been too smooth up until this time. I mean, there had been no Sheriff's Deputy coming after us, no Coast Guard Cutter boarding us, no mega-yacht wanting to raft up with us, well, you get the picture. So, this must be the new approach. The chopper set down, but never killed the motor. A lone figure disembarked duffel bag in hand and headed our way at a jog. Essie and I both recognized the passenger before he got to our section of the docks. He jogged over to us and stopped right alongside. Essie spoke first.

"Jim Grimshaw, what a nice surprise. You coming to see us off?"

"Well, not exactly."

It seemed that everything that had happened to us recently started with a line like that. I waited for the other shoe to fall.

"Captain Les. Bob Leisey was telling me what a wonderful time he had on Calypso. He indicated that you might want a hand to replace him."

"Is that right?"

"Well, he thought you might, anyway. Listen, I need to get away for a little while. Several of my ex's are after new deals, trying to serve papers constantly. I've got some time before my next picture starts filming and I'd really like to have a little down time to read the script, just look at the water, be a regular person. I'm tired and need a change. What do you say? I'll help with expenses and pull my weight. No special privileges expected."

Essie looked at me like, why the Hell not?

"Jim, listen, I don't have a problem with you coming along. But, we're a little worn out ourselves and have been having almost too much excitement recently. You sure we won't have helicopters overhead with photographers wanting to shoot us all in the nude? I mean, I don't want to wind up in the National Enquirer. I've got an ex-wife also who ain't even an official "ex" yet. She doesn't need any ammunition. You understand my concern?"

"Captain Les, I promise, you take me along for several weeks, maybe till we get to the Keys, or the Bahamas, and I will only be a help to you. It will be the most relaxing sail you ever had. I've sailed a little and I'm not afraid to dive in, so to speak."

"OK, Jim, you're the new First Mate, come-aboard."

"I have to tell you though, you had me scared for a minute. I just knew something weird was about to happen."

"Hey, not with me. Maybe Tom Cruise or Arnold or some other actors lead above the line lives, but I'm just a regular guy."

Grimshaw and I threw the dock-lines onto the finger pier and we started our journey south. I guess that maybe an hour had passed before Grimshaw queried.

"Are we going to be able to stop in Jackonville to pick up Demi? She can bunk with me, and I promise, everything will be just as simple and ordinary as I promised. And, can I hook up my laptop to the VHF? Just to check my e-mail?"

I don't know why I ever thought this was going to be simple, looking for the perfect place, the perfect palm. Our adventure with John Silver, yeah that's how we like to think of him, was just the first of many to come. Grimshaw was about to make the experience with John Silver seem like a short nap in church.

The End -

for now.

To order Volume Two (Conclusion) of

The Sea Les Traveled

please complete the order form below.

Volume　　ONE　or　TWO　(Circle correct volume)

Number of copies desired: _____

Name:_____

Address:

Street or PO Box_____

City and State: _____

Zip Code:_____

Would you like this autographed?　Yes/No

To Whom:_____

Phone:_____

Send $19.95 US and this page to:

ESSIE PRESS

P.O. Box 6684

Raleigh, North Carolina 27628-6684

Or

visit our Website: <lespendleton.com>